D1525232

ANTONIO

ANTONIO

TEXAS BOUDREAU BROTHERHOOD

By
KATHY IVAN

COPYRIGHT

Antonio – Original Copyright © March 2020 by Kathy Ivan

Cover by Elizabeth Mackay of EMGRAPHICS

Release date: March 2020
Print Edition

All Rights Reserved

This book is a work of fiction. Names, places, characters and incidents are the product of the author's imagination or are fictionally used. Any resemblance to actual events, locales, or persons living or dead is coincidental.

No part of this book may be reproduced, downloaded, transmitted, decompiled, reverse engineered, stored in or introduced to any information storage and retrieval system, in any form, whether electronic or mechanical without the author's written permission. Scanning, uploading or distribution of this book via the Internet or any other means without permission is prohibited.

ANTONIO – Texas Boudreau Brotherhood

Tasked with locating a missing government witness, FBI agent Antonio Boudreau jumps at the chance to work closer to his home town of Shiloh Springs, Texas. Ever since somebody tried to kill her while under the feds protection, Serena Snowden's been on the lam. Serena holds the key to defeating a homegrown terrorist, but can Antonio keep her alive long enough to use it?

BOOKS BY KATHY IVAN

www.kathyivan.com/books.html

TEXAS BOUDREAU BROTHERHOOD
Rafe

Antonio

Brody

NEW ORLEANS CONNECTION SERIES
Desperate Choices

Connor's Gamble

Relentless Pursuit

Ultimate Betrayal

Keeping Secrets

Sex, Lies and Apple Pies

Deadly Justice

Wicked Obsession

Hidden Agenda

Spies Like Us

Fatal Intentions

New Orleans Connection Series Box Set: Books 1-3

New Orleans Connection Series Box Set: Books 4-7

CAJUN CONNECTION SERIES
Saving Sarah

Saving Savannah

Saving Stephanie

Guarding Gabi

Dear Reader,

Welcome to Shiloh Springs, Texas! Don't you just love a small Texas town, where the people are neighborly, the gossip plentiful, and the heroes are …well, heroic, not to mention easy on the eyes! I love everything about Texas, which I why I've made the great state my home for over thirty years. There's no other place like it. From the delicious Tex-Mex food and downhome barbecue, the majestic scenery, and friendly atmosphere, the people and places of the Lone Star state are as unique and colorful as you'll find anywhere.

The Texas Boudreau Brotherhood series centers around a group of foster brothers, men who would have ended up in the system if not for Douglas and Patricia Boudreau. Instead of being hardened by life and circumstances beyond their control, they found a family who loved and accepted them, and gave them a place to call home. Sometimes brotherhood is more than sharing the same DNA.

If you've read my other romantic suspense books (the New Orleans Connection series and Cajun Connection series), you'll be familiar with the Boudreau name. Turns out there are a whole lot of Boudreaus out there, just itching to have their stories told. (Douglas is the brother of Gator Boudreau, patriarch of the New Orleans branch of the Boudreau family.)

So, sit back and relax. The pace of small-living might be less hectic than the big city, but small towns hold secrets, excitement, and heroes to ride to the rescue. And who doesn't love a Texas cowboy?

Kathy Ivan

EDITORIAL REVIEWS

"Kathy Ivan's books are addictive, you can't read just one."

—Susan Stoker, NYT Bestselling Author

"Kathy Ivan's books give you everything you're looking for and so much more."

—Geri Foster, USA Today and NYT Bestselling Author of the Falcon Securities Series

"In Shiloh Springs, Kathy Ivan has crafted warm, engaging characters that will steal your heart and a mystery that will keep you reading to the very last page."

—Barb Han, *USA TODAY* and Publisher's Weekly Bestselling Author

"This is the first I have read from Kathy Ivan and it won't be the last."

—Night Owl Reviews

"I highly recommend Desperate Choices. Readers can't go wrong here!"

—Melissa, Joyfully Reviewed

"I loved how the author wove a very intricate storyline with plenty of intriguing details that led to the final reveal…"

—Night Owl Reviews

Desperate Choices—Winner 2012 International Digital Award—Suspense

Desperate Choices—Best of Romance 2011 –Joyfully Reviewed

DEDICATIONS AND ACKNOWLEDGEMENTS

To my sister, Mary Sullivan, for her unwavering belief that I can write good stories. She is always there, helping me, encouraging me, and generally doing whatever it takes to get the writing done. Trust me, if she wasn't there prodding me, the books might never be finished. And I always dedicate books to my mother, Betty Sullivan. Her love of reading and sharing that love for books, no matter the genre, set me on the path to storytelling. She instilled in me the joy of reading at an early age and a love of romance. I'd also like to thank Chris Keniston and Barb Han, and our weekly portal calls, for keeping me accountable and determined to get the book written. Sometimes it's not easy, but with good friends helping and supporting me, I can do anything! And a special shout out to all the readers, who keep me going. Knowing that you enjoy my books and want more, there's no greater feeling in the world.

More about Kathy and her books can be found at

WEBSITE:
www.kathyivan.com

Follow Kathy on Facebook at
www.facebook.com/kathyivanauthor

Follow Kathy on Twitter at
twitter.com/@kathyivan

Follow Kathy at BookBub
bookbub.com/profile/kathy-ivan

NEWSLETTER SIGN UP

Don't want to miss out on any new books, contests, and free stuff? Sign up to get my newsletter. I promise not to spam you, and only send out notifications/e-mails whenever there's a new release or contest/giveaway. Follow the link and join today!

http://eepurl.com/baqdRX

ANTONIO

By
KATHY IVAN

CHAPTER ONE

The pages of the slick glossy magazine taunted her, laying poised smack dab in the middle of her desk. The sight sent a shiver of dread down Serena Snowden's spine. Everyone in the office had been over the moon when a national interior design magazine contacted the real estate company's owner, Patti Boudreau, about being part of a spread featuring the top twenty-five best real estate companies in the country, and Boudreau Realty made the short list. Although a fairly small real estate company by national standards, heck, even by Texas standards, mention of the company in its prestigious pages was a big deal, and Ms. Patti deserved all the credit. She treated her agents and realtors with honesty and respect, and Serena adored her mentor. But, she'd deliberately skipped out of the photo shoot the day the photographer came to highlight their company.

Why did it feel like an alien lifeform was currently trying to claw its way out of the pit of her stomach? There was no way—absolutely no way—the photographer from the magazine captured a picture of her. Even if they had, what were the odds of it making it into the magazine? Surely they wouldn't post pictures of all twenty-five realty companies and their associates? The magazine's interior was prime real estate. If anything, the pics would be small, the people unrecognizable—she hoped.

"Did you see our picture, Serena?" Elizabeth Burkette, office manager for Boudreau Realty, perched on the chair across from Serena's desk, practically vibrating with excitement. "They only used five pictures for the entire article, and we're one! Isn't it awesome?"

"Awesome," Serena echoed, reaching for the magazine with a trembling hand. She wanted to pick it up as much as she wanted to grab a rattlesnake by the head, but Elizabeth sat on the edge of the chair, a huge grin on her face, waiting for her to look. Every instinct screamed for her to flee, and she swallowed down the bile in her throat, before picking up the glossy magazine.

"I marked the page for you with a sticky note."

"Thanks, Elizabeth." Drawing in a deep breath, she opened the magazine, her eyes scanning the page, focusing on each photo. Near the bottom, in bold brilliant color, Boudreau Realty was displayed. It was one of those candid-type shots, where people sat at their desks or at the file cabinets, instead of a posed group pic. Releasing the breath she'd been holding, she looked at Elizabeth and smiled. Everything was good. Serena wasn't in the picture.

"The one on the bottom is good, but I meant the one on

the top of the next page." Elizabeth stood and leaned across the desk, tapping her finger on the picture at the top of the opposite page. Serena's breath caught in her throat. She felt lightheaded at the sight of her, Elizabeth, and Ms. Patti standing beside the copier. They looked to be having an animated discussion, and Serena held a sheaf of papers in her left hand. *How was this possible?* She'd been so darned careful, made sure she and the photographer hadn't been in the office at the same time.

"I can't believe my picture is in a national magazine! My sister is going to have kittens when she sees this."

"Here." Serena pasted a smile on her face and handed the magazine to Elizabeth, her heartbeat racing, bile churning in her stomach. "Take mine so you'll have an extra one."

"Are you sure? Don't you want a copy? I mean, you're in there too." Despite her words, Elizabeth snagged the magazine and clutched it to her chest.

"It's fine. Keep it." Serena stood, pulling her purse from the bottom drawer of her desk, and slung the strap over her shoulder. She took a long look around her desk, the realization sinking in she probably wouldn't see it again after today. Turning away so Elizabeth wouldn't see her tearing up, she gave herself a mental shake.

Get it together. You knew you'd have to leave eventually. It's not safe to stay in one place too long.

"I'm running late. I've got an appointment to show a couple of rental properties. Can you let Ms. Patti know I'll give her a call later tonight?" Serena grabbed the manila folder from her inbox and shoved it into her purse, the one she carried everything in, not caring if the pages got wrinkled and mutilated in the process. She needed to get out. Away from the office, someplace where she could draw breath and figure out her next move.

Staying in Shiloh Springs was no longer an option. Not once the magazine hit the shelves. If anybody in her family caught wind of where she lived—well, it didn't matter, because she wouldn't be living much longer if they found her.

Every instinct screamed for her to run, jump in her car and drive, without a backward glance. Leave everything behind. Starting over was hard, but she'd done it before, and she could do it again. Nobody in Shiloh Springs knew who she really was; they knew the persona she'd adopted the last time she'd moved, trying to stay one step ahead of her uncle and his followers after they'd found her before. Tears burned her eyes as she fumbled with her keys, dropping them on the ground at her feet.

"Crap." Squatting down, her hand wrapped around the key fob. Clutching it in her fist, she drew in a deep breath. It wasn't the end of the world, just the end of this phase of her life of changing identities and running away from her troubles. Everything would work out, though right now her heart was breaking to leave it all behind. She'd been so sure this time was different, hoping she had a chance at a normal life.

Looks like I was wrong.

"Everything okay, Serena?"

Time froze at the sound of his voice. Antonio Boudreau. What was he doing here? She hadn't known Antonio was in Shiloh Springs. Last she heard, he'd headed back to Dallas after everything calmed down with the whole Rafe and Tessa scandal, a fiasco which nearly ended up killing the school-teacher and the county sheriff. Fortunately, things worked out and they were blissfully happy. She wouldn't be surprised if there weren't wedding bells in their future.

"Antonio, you startled me." She straightened, holding up the keys. "A case of butterfingers. I'm late for an appointment."

His dark eyes studied her intently, and she ducked her head, refusing to meet his direct stare. Sharp as a tack and adept at reading people better than anybody she knew, she didn't dare let on anything was amiss. He'd get suspicious and go into Mr. FBI agent mode, sticking his nose into her business. It was the last thing she could afford to happen now, not when she stood on the brink of her whole world imploding.

"Okay." He drawled out the word, still watching her closely, a tiny smile playing on his lips. "Thought I'd stop by and say hello. I'm headed to Austin. The Dallas office is loaning me out to help on a case, because they're short-staffed. I don't mind, it gives me a chance to be a little closer to home, which is always nice."

"That's great. I'm sure Douglas and Ms. Patti will love you're being able to visit more often." She pressed the button on the key fob, unlocking the door and pulled it open, tossing her bag onto the passenger seat. "Sorry, I've gotta go. My client is waiting for me."

"Of course. I'll see you later." He stepped back, making room for her to inch past him. Her shoulder brushed his arm as she scooted past, and her breath caught in her throat. *Why, why, why did this have to happen now? Antonio's finally going to be around Shiloh Springs more, which is what I've always wanted, and I've got to run—again.*

As she drove away, her gaze strayed to the rearview mirror. Antonio stood still as a statue in the parking lot, his eyes watching her, his expression serious yet unreadable. She kept her eyes glued to him silhouetted in the mirror until he disappeared from view, trying to memorize the sight. One last memory of the man who'd fascinated her from the moment they'd met. Another regret to add to the list of things she wished she could change. Swallowing back a sigh, she headed for her townhouse to pack.

Antonio stared as the car pulled away, arms crossed over his chest. Well, that had been strange. Nothing about his encounter with Serena felt normal. She'd been flustered and jumpy, almost skittish. Not the woman he'd known for almost a year. Tugging on the brim of his cowboy hat, he debated going into the real estate office and saying hello to his mother. He'd be lying if he said the only reason he'd stopped by Boudreau Reality had been to visit with family. Catching a glimpse of the dark-haired beauty who'd skedaddled away as though her tail was on fire might've played a significant part in his detour.

Glancing at his watch, he realized it was later than he thought. He'd have to call his momma from the road, because he needed to check in with the Austin office before the end of the day and get a quick briefing on the case he'd be working. Come morning, he could hit the ground running. He'd been feeling stifled in Dallas, the big city closing in on him, suffocating any pleasure he got from doing the job he'd always loved. It hadn't taken him long to realize he wasn't meant for big city living, but once there, he'd been kinda stuck. Maybe this change of location, being a lot closer to Shiloh Springs and his family, could help him make the hard decisions about his life and what he wanted to do with it.

With one last look in the direction Serena had driven away, he shook his head and climbed into his car. Figuring her out would have to wait. He had a job to do.

CHAPTER TWO

Serena parked in the driveway of Ms. Patti's house, known throughout Shiloh Springs as the Big House, and shut off the engine. Even though the Boudreaus had lived here for generations, nobody called the Boudreau ranch anything but the Big House, and the name stuck. She loved the place, and was going to miss being able to spend time out here in the country, breathing in the sweet, clean air and the feeling of home she always got whenever she stepped foot on the land.

As much as she wanted to scurry away under cover of darkness, telling nobody why she'd left or where she was heading, she couldn't do that to Ms. Patti. The woman had been more than a mentor to her since she stumbled into Shiloh Springs almost a year ago. Ms. Patti had become a surrogate mother, replacing the one she barely remembered. Her biological mother had left when she was a little girl, barely able to remember what she looked like, and her father remarried not long after and had spent all his time catering to his new wife. That is when he wasn't sitting in Big Jim's pocket or bowing and scraping to please his former brother-in-law.

Now it was time to say goodbye and leave the town and the people she'd come to love behind, and never look back. She closed her eyes to stop the tears welling up. Blinking rapidly, she brushed her fingers over her eyelids and took a deep breath. This wasn't the time to fall apart. It could wait until she hit the road, leaving Shiloh Springs in her rearview mirror.

Staring through the windshield, she studied the Boudreau home. It was perfect, and she loved this ranch and everything about it. A huge white-painted house, it epitomized everything she secretly wished for with its simple, elegant style. Two stories tall, it sported huge wraparound porches, one on each level. Dark green shutters flanked the large windows on each side, their color a stark, yet inviting contrast to the brilliant white. A single-story addition had been added to the east side of the house at some point over the years and sported a rooftop deck. She knew the master bedroom suite on the second floor held French doors opening onto the rooftop escape, surrounded by a white railing which mirrored the design of the ones encircling the massive twin porches. It embodied the perfect place for early morning coffee and getting ready for the upcoming day, or to sit back with a good book and a cup of tea in the evening after a hectic day at the office.

A large red brick chimney rose over the roofline, and a long front walkway of matching brick tied everything together, painting a homey picture. Sprawling live oak trees flanked each side of the house, adding character and grace to an already perfect picture.

A wave of envy pierced her as she imagined settling into a home like this, knowing it could never happen. People like her didn't end up with the fairy-tale ending, the handsome prince, or the happily ever after.

Climbing from the car, she walked to the front door, running her hand along the balustrade surrounding the porch. The white paint was starting to show a bit of age, its creamy patina adding another layer of warmth to the tableau tugging at her heartstrings. She was going to miss sweet tea on Saturday afternoons with Ms. Patti. They'd made it their own personal ritual, a way to catch up on everything going on in the office during the week, and spend a little quality time together.

"Don't just stand there, girl, come on in." Douglas Boudreau held the front door open and motioned her inside. Towering over her by several inches, and built like a mountain, most people were intimated by the blunt older man, but she'd found him to be a pussycat. A gentle giant with a heart of gold.

"Thanks, Douglas. I'm here to see Ms. Patti." She stood on tiptoe and kissed his cheek, watching the blush creep into his face at her gesture of affection. Douglas always made her feel welcomed and appreciated in his home, and from the stories she'd heard about the Boudreaus when she'd first moved to Shiloh Springs, knew he didn't suffer fools, and was a fierce protector of his family, especially the boys they'd welcomed in their home over the years. She was going to miss him.

"She's in the kitchen. You can head on back." He placed a meaty hand on her shoulder and gave it a squeeze before heading out the front door. Steeling herself, she headed through the hallway to the kitchen and paused in the opening.

"Ms. Patti, I—"

"Sit down, hon. We need to talk." Although Ms. Patti's back was to her, Serena read the tension in the way she held her shoulders, and the ramrod straightness of her spine. Heck, she hadn't even told Ms. Patti why she needed to speak with her when she'd called, but somehow the older woman knew. And she wasn't a happy camper.

"I'm sorry for showing up early like this. But, I wanted— no, needed to tell you in person I'm leaving. I'm sorry for the short notice."

"Serena, sit down before you fall down. I knew something was wrong when you called last night. I didn't want to push, figured you tell me when you were ready. Now, you show up and tell me you're leaving?"

Serena felt lower than a caterpillar crawling under a doorframe. The hurt in Ms. Patti's voice, the disappointment in her face nearly undid her resolve. She wanted to stay, but that option was closed. If she stayed, not only would her uncle find her, she'd be putting her friends' lives in jeopardy. Big Jim Berkley wouldn't care about collateral damage, not if it meant catching up and eliminating Serena. As far as he was concerned, she was a traitor to her family, and deserved to be put down like a mongrel dog. The threats he'd spewed in the courtroom after the reading of the verdict still rang in her ears, and she knew to the depths of her soul he meant every word.

"Ms. Patti, you know I've loved working in Shiloh Springs, and you've been the best boss I've ever had, but it's time for me to head out."

"What are your plans, hon? You know I'll give you a reference. You've been an asset to the office, at least until you've thrown this monkey wrench into the mix. I can tell something's wrong." Ms. Patti placed her hand atop Serena's, leaning in closer. "You can talk to me, you know, right? Anything you say, I'll never repeat. You're white as a sheet, and shaking like a leaf. Tell me what's wrong, and I'll fix it."

Serena gave a shaky laugh. Ms. Patti did love to fix things for the people she loved. If anybody had a problem, all they had to do was tell Ms. Patti and poof, problem solved. Only this wasn't a problem she could wave her magic wand at and make it go away. So, she did the only thing she could do. She lied.

"Nothing's wrong. I told you in the beginning, when you hired me, I'm a nomad. A gypsy who doesn't put down roots. Staying in one place too long gives me the heebie-jeebies. My itchy feet tell me it's time to move along, start a new adventure."

Ms. Patti studied her intently, her stare seeming to see straight into her soul. The feeling she was being weighed in the balance. After several excruciating long seconds, Ms. Patti smiled.

"There are a lot of ways to curb wanderlust that don't involve uprooting your life. Taking a vacation. Going on an adventure. Start a new hobby. Don't lie to yourself or to me about why you're leaving. You're scared. Running from something or somebody in your past. I've known it from the start. I recognized all the signs and hired you anyway, even with your lack of experience because I could tell, deep down, you needed someplace to call home."

Serena opened her mouth to deny Ms. Patti's words, then closed it because she was right. She didn't know who or what Serena was running from, but the desire to find one place where she could stop, even if for a short time, had tempted her like a siren's song. Her fake ID gave her a realtor's license, and on a whim, she'd walked through the doors of Boudreau Realty, and met the amazing woman across from her, who'd taken a chance on her.

"Home is wherever I lay my head at night."

Ms. Patti leaned back in her chair, a curious smile on her lips. "You remind me so much of my boys. Every one of them came here with the same attitude, the same 'I don't need anybody or anything to be happy' mentality. Like them, you're struggling to find your place. You're scared of opening up and caring about other people because you've been hurt. Serena, we've all been hurt at one point or another. I could tell you stories about my past that would have you bawling like a baby in five minutes. Every one of my sons have pasts, some more horrific than others, but they all needed a soft place to land. A place where they could find their balance, and be able to grow roots and hold their heads up."

Serena crossed her arms across her chest, bracing herself against the words. She couldn't fall into this trap, because it was one. A deep cavern of sharp, pointy rocks waiting to devour her if she took one wrong step. Someone had befriended her when she first went into witness protection, and she'd believed she was safe to start a new life, have friends, maybe even find love. He'd ended up with his throat slit, simply because he was her friend. Ms. Patti, Douglas, all of the Boudreaus meant even more to her. If she listened, if she stayed, the possibility of them being in danger was an intolerable thought. She was making the right decision.

"No, you're making the wrong decision," Ms. Patti answered, as if reading her mind. "Whatever inner demon is chasing you will never stop, not unless or until you take a stand. Face it head on and don't give in. I am here, and I'll stand by your side, and help you fight. Douglas will too. You're not alone."

Could she do it? Staying in Shiloh Springs held a greater appeal than setting out on the road, looking for a new place to hide. Always looking over her shoulder, wondering if the next person she met might be the last. She wasn't even certain her uncle knew where she was; there hadn't been any indication he'd read the article or seen the photo.

It was a risk, but at the end of the day wasn't the reward worth taking a chance? Antonio's face popped into her thoughts, with his handsome dark looks, the Italian elegance of his profile and his cocky smile. Leaving him behind would be leaving a piece of herself behind too, because she'd come to care about him more than was safe.

"Okay, Ms. Patti. I'll give it a shot, but I can't make any promises. I've always given in when the urge to move on hits. It might become too much, and I'll head out for parts unknown. I've always wanted to travel abroad, maybe I'll look into going to Italy."

Why did I mention Italy? I need to stop thinking with my heart, and listen to my head.

A tiny smile curved Ms. Patti's lips, and Serena knew she hadn't fooled the older woman one iota. She'd gotten her way, and Serena hoped nobody ended up paying for her decision.

"Good, it's settled. Now, let's get down to business. What's going on with the Rudiger place? Any prospects?"

And just like that, Serena's world felt right again. She prayed Big Jim never found out about Shiloh Springs.

CHAPTER THREE

"**G**lad to have you here, Boudreau." Special Agent in Charge Derrick Williamson leaned back in his chair, his hands clasped across his stomach. Antonio studied the man, took in the freshly pressed shirt, suit pants. The top button of Williamson's shirt was undone and his tie loosened, giving off a casual vibe, but Antonio didn't buy it, not for a second.

At first glance, Williamson portrayed the easygoing, overworked FBI agent to a tee, but Antonio never went with what was obvious to the naked eye. He'd long ago learned taking things at face value often led to big mistakes, a lesson he'd vowed never to repeat. Williamson appeared fit, his sandy-brown hair cut short in a businessman style. He looked like he worked out regularly, and didn't have the paunch across his middle most pencil pushers seemed to gain working in an office.

An off-white cowboy hat lay on the credenza behind Williamson, as though it had been taken off and tossed onto the surface cluttered with papers and files. Now that he could believe. Most everybody in Texas wouldn't be caught dead without their hat.

"Happy to be here. What can you tell me about the case?" He eased onto the chair opposite the desk, and propped his foot on the opposite knee, resting his own cowboy hat there. "Sounds like you've got your hands full down here."

Williamson sighed. "You've got no idea, Boudreau. Two agents out with gunshot wounds. One on maternity leave. One ruptured appendix. And two more who relocated to different cities. Leaving us in a mighty big hole we're still trying to dig our way out of. Which is why I'm glad you're here, even if it's temporary."

Looking closer, Antonio noted the dark circles under Williamson's eyes, the slightly grayish pallor to his skin. The man was obviously running on fumes, never a good idea when dealing with high profile cases or even the small stuff. A tired agent missed things.

Williamson tossed a folder across his desk. "This one's been a pain in my backside for months. How familiar are you with James "Big Jim" Berkley?"

Antonio's brow rose at the mention of the name. Big Jim Berkley's case had been on the FBI list for years, until he'd finally been arrested, tried, and convicted two years earlier. Headline on the nightly news on every news station for months, the scandal of infighting within his family, plus the nature of his crimes provided fodder for the press, and the viewing public ate it up, spreading it across television stations until you couldn't change the channel without somebody talking about the bombings.

"I remember when he was arrested. Wasn't he caught in San Antonio? Liked to bomb synagogues, mosques, any place where minorities and people with different ideologies congregated."

Williamson leaned back in his chair, and ran a hand through his hair. "That's him alright. The man is charismatic and has a following still active to this day. Most members of his family are part of his whacked out cult. Has a bunch of rabid believers who hang on every word the idiot spouts."

Cocking his head, Antonio opened the file, and stared at the picture of James Berkley. The man was big, at least six three, maybe six four, two-hundred and fifty pounds, and it looked like it was all muscle. Salt and pepper hair. He couldn't tell from the black-and-white picture what color his eyes were, but they were cold. Empty.

"Why is the FBI looking at Berkley again? Isn't he in federal prison serving multiple life sentences?" Antonio's eyes scanned the front page of the file, and he straightened when he noted the words "appeal granted". "This can't be right. He's getting an appeal? There was a ton of evidence against him. No way does this guy walk."

"His attorneys found some loophole, and he's trying to scurry through it like the filthy little weasel he is. At least the courts are keeping him in prison for now, until the appeal's been heard. But we've got another problem." Williamson's tone filled with disgust. "Berkley's niece was the backbone of the government's case. She provided a good chunk of the evidence used to convict Berkley. Her testimony nailed his coffin good and tight. Before the trial, she was guarded day and night. Afterwards, she went into witness protection."

Antonio quickly put two and two together, and tossed the file on the chair next to him. "Lemme guess. Berkley put a hit out on the niece to shut her up. If she can't testify, the feds case dries up, right?"

"Pretty much. Berkley's had people searching for Sharon since before the first trial. The government kept a tight lid on her throughout and whisked her away the minute she'd finished testifying, even before the verdict came down. But somehow her location was leaked and Berkley's hired goons found her in Las Vegas."

Antonio felt a clenching sensation in his gut. "She's dead?"

Williamson shook his head. "Don't know. Her next-door neighbor ended up dead and Sharon Berkley disappeared. Vanished without a trace. Witness protection searched for months, examined every trail, every whisper of a lead, but either Berkley had her taken out—which is possible, and he's kept his mouth shut about it—or she's good enough to stay under the radar. My gut tells me Berkley's still looking for her, because I doubt he'd be able to shut up about it if he'd had her eliminated. He's too vain and thinks he's smarter than everybody involved in his case. No, we going under the assumption she's alive and hiding."

Antonio drummed his fingertips against his knee, his mind sorting through the information Williamson shared. It made sense Sharon Berkley could still be alive. But it was hard to stay completely off the grid in this day and age of electronic surveillance, computers, and facial recognition software. If she was out there, they'd find her. He only hoped it was before Big Jim Berkley did.

"What specifics can you tell me about Sharon Berkley? Last known whereabouts, any information from WITSEC? Or am I overstepping? I figure since you're telling me about Berkley's case, you want me to help locate her?"

Williamson picked up another folder and shoved it across the desk. Antonio bit back a chuckle at the disgruntled look on the other man's face. He had a feeling he'd get along well with Williamson, once they'd worked out the initial posturing that always happened when two alpha dogs went after the same bone. Didn't matter, he was only here temporarily anyway. He'd try not to yank Williamson's tail too hard.

"Like I said, she was initially relocated to Vegas. Worked a menial job in a veterinarian's office. Lived in a quiet suburb outside downtown, in a small two-bedroom townhouse. Mostly kept to herself. Rarely dated. About four months after the trial ended, police responded to an alarm at her townhouse. When they got there, she was in the wind. Next door neighbor found with his throat slit. Local cops think he interrupted an attempted robbery, since her screens were cut and a window broken. They don't know if Sharon was home at the time, because they never talked to her. She vanished like a puff of smoke."

"Hmm. You're thinking Big Jim sent somebody after her. You mentioned a leak. Any idea who?"

"Yeah. Said hole has since been plugged, but WITSEC is still cleaning up the fallout from their fiasco."

"And nobody's heard from Sharon Berkley since Vegas?"

Williamson leaned forward and picked up the coffee mug from his desk, and took a deep drink. "Two days after the neighbor's murder, she contacted the agent assigned to her case. Terrified and unsure who to trust, she drove for hours before holing up in a roach coach motel on the outskirts of Denver."

Antonio nodded. "That's actually pretty smart. Put some distance between her and the thugs out to get her. At least she didn't try to hide from the government, at least not right away. I'm going to assume they moved her again to a new location, new ID, the whole shebang."

"Witness protection got her out, relocated her to Lincoln, Nebraska. She worked in a mall. Not the most glamorous job, but easy enough she could get lost in a crowd if needed. But the next hired assassin found her easy enough. Too easy, if you ask me, but then I don't work for WITSEC." Antonio could almost hear the silently added, *because if I did this sure as heck wouldn't have happened.*

He held the still unopened file on Sharon Berkley in his hand, wanting to hear everything Williamson knew before digging into the case. The agent seemed to have a good head on his shoulders, and a lot of insight into a case Antonio wasn't completely familiar with, other than what he'd seen on the evening news or what he'd read in the press, and even then it had been a couple of years ago. Firsthand knowledge always added intriguing layers to a case, giving a perspective to things which might otherwise be overlooked.

"Sharon Berkley worked on the second floor at the mall, having earned her way up to store manager for a lingerie shop. Took a lunch break and headed for the food court to grab a bite. Somehow she ended up going head first over the railing and landed on the first floor. Witnesses couldn't say for sure what happened, but Sharon told the police at the hospital she'd been pushed." Williamson took another drink of his coffee, before continuing. "The police report on the incident's in your file. Officer taking her statement at the hospital said she seemed jumpy and nervous, flinched at the slightest noise. No broken bones, but a badly sprained wrist and lots of bruising. Doctors were concerned she had a concussion, and insisted she be kept overnight."

"Lemme guess," Antonio quipped. "She disappeared from the hospital."

"Bingo. Sometime between four a.m. and six a.m. when the nurse went to check on her, she'd ghosted. Never went back to her apartment. Left her purse and all her belongings behind at the hospital, right down to the clothes she wore.

The hospital was missing one pair of scrubs. Security footage showed her exiting through the loading dock at four fifty-seven. She was limping, wrist bandaged and her arm in a sling, but she hightailed it out to the parking lot and disappeared off the camera. This time she didn't contact WITSEC, and nobody has heard from her. At all. The identity she'd been given in Vegas and the one she'd been using in Lincoln have had no activity since. She hasn't been spotted on any facial recognition software at airports, train stations or bus stations. In other words, we have no clue where to find her. It's like she's vanished into thin air."

"So, basically, nobody has seen Sharon Berkley for what, at least two years?"

Williamson nodded. "Give or take a few months."

Antonio stood, still holding the file on Sharon Berkley and picked up his hat and the file on James Berkley. "Got a place for me to spread out and work?"

Williamson stood and walked around his desk. "Check with Michelle, the woman who showed you in. She'll get you set up at a desk and make sure you have computer access for whatever you need." He paused and met Antonio's gaze. "We have to find Sharon Berkley. Nobody's safe if Big Jim Berkley is walking the streets a free man. She's the only one who can assure we put him away for good."

Drawing in a deep breath, Antonio tapped the folders. "I'll find her."

Williamson slapped him lightly on the back. "Welcome to Austin, Boudreau."

CHAPTER FOUR

Early morning at Daisy's Diner meant wading through the crowds to find an empty table. And she was late, because Serena had barely slept a wink the night before. She still hadn't figured out why she'd let Ms. Patti talk her into staying in Shiloh Springs. Then again, most folks didn't say no to Patti Boudreau. The woman was a force of nature, sweeping everyone along in her wake. Serena's eyes scanned the diner, finally spotting the group she'd come to meet at a table about halfway toward the back.

Tessa Maxwell waved, motioning her forward, and Serena maneuvered between the chairs and the booths against the wall, until she slid into the last empty seat at the table. "Morning, ladies."

"Good morning, sunshine." Without a word, Tessa grabbed the coffee carafe and filled Serena's cup. *Thank goodness.* Serena wasn't a morning person, preferring to sleep in whenever she could, especially on the weekends. Getting up while it was still dark outside meant she wasn't a happy camper on the best of days, especially when she hadn't had her caffeine charge, but today she felt extra growly. Stirring in some sugar, she took a sip and moaned as the warmth seeped deep into her bones.

"I may have to worship at Daisy's feet. I swear the woman makes a mean pot of coffee." She took another sip and gave a contented sigh. "I see y'all started without me." Each woman had a plate in front of them, loaded with breakfast foods. Now she had some life-saving coffee in her system, the smells of bacon and sausage, pancakes, and cinnamon buns hit her. Darn it, somehow with all the drama yesterday, she'd forgotten to eat. No wonder she felt lightheaded and surly.

"Hi, Serena! What can I get you?" Daisy stood across from her, a smile lighting her face. Although she had to be running herself ragged, judging from the crowded diner, she seemed to bubble with energy. Serena smiled at the sapphire-blue streaks Daisy had added into her blonde hair. They were quirky and fun, like the woman standing before her with an order pad in her hand. Not that she needed it. She couldn't remember a single time she'd come in when Daisy messed up an order. When it came to the diner, her pride and joy, Daisy never missed a beat.

"Diet's going out the window this morning. I'll have a stack of pancakes with a side of bacon, and a glass of O.J."

"You got it. Be right back." Daisy practically bounced toward the counter, pausing to chat with a customer before heading to the large open window to place Serena's order. Before Serena even had time to finish her coffee, Daisy was back with her juice.

"I've only got a minute, because things are crazy busy this morning as you can see, so I can't chat too long. What's up with y'all?" Daisy leaned over Tessa's shoulder, keeping her voice low. "Anything interesting happening I should know about? It's been so nuts around here, I feel like I'm missing out on all the good gossip."

Jill Monroe shook her head. "Same old, same old with me. Work's driving me bonkers. Boss is an idiot. I swear, it's a miracle he can tie his own shoes." Glancing down at her plate, she stabbed at the sausage patty, and Serena cringed at the poor, unfortunate soul who'd inspired Jill's ire. They'd better watch out. Jill might be small in stature, but she was fierce when pissed off, and apparently her boss was stepping on her last nerve.

Beth Stewart, Tessa's sister, smiled shyly. Beth wasn't a Shiloh Springs local; instead she was visiting her sister for a much-needed break. Tessa had urged the other ladies at the table to befriend Beth, because she was still suffering from the aftershocks of her now ex-husband's actions. Serena couldn't imagine the anguish Beth suffered, knowing the man she'd married, the father of her child, tried to kill her sister, and had planned to kill her too.

"I've got nothing." Serena picked up her juice. "Thought I had a big fish on the hook, but he decided Shiloh Springs' small town charm wasn't 'right' for their new store. Sometimes you can't teach idiots, especially when they're wrong."

Daisy shrugged. "Their loss. We are awesome." Her

words were accompanied with a cheeky grin and a waggle of her eyebrows.

Serena glanced at Tessa then, since she was the last woman and hadn't chimed in. Oh, yeah, she was definitely hiding something, though she didn't seem upset, more like— excited. "Okay, Miss Schoolmarm, spill it. You're vibrating with the need to talk. Go for it."

Tessa rolled her eyes, then stuck out her tongue, and Serena made a playful swat at her. "Wow, talk about stealing my thunder. I planned on waiting until we'd finished breakfast, but here goes." Lifting her hand from under the edge of the table, she turned it, spotlighting the diamond on her left ring finger. "Rafe asked me to marry him."

Loud squeals erupted from the women seated at the table, and Daisy grabbed Tessa in a hug, since she was closest to her. "Oh, sugar, congratulations!" she beamed. "I guess this means you're staying in Shiloh Springs permanently."

Tessa chuckled. "I guess it does."

"Congratulations, Tessa! I'm happy for you." Serena meant her heartfelt words. She remembered the day she'd met the feisty redhead. On the day Tessa moved to Shiloh Springs, as her realtor, Serena had an appointment to meet her at the house Tessa had rented, to drop off the keys and copies of the lease. Running late and without a number to contact her, instead Rafe Boudreau caught Tessa climbing through the window in the now infamous bathroom break-in story, which he took great glee in repeating to anybody who'd listen. Instantaneous and undeniable chemistry between the two exploded and hadn't dimmed one iota since, and Serena remained convinced they'd be happy together. How could they not, they were perfect for each other.

Several minutes were spent examining the beautiful sapphire and diamond engagement ring on Tessa's left hand, and Serena had to admit it suited Tessa perfectly. Rafe had made a good choice.

"If y'all need anything, gimme a holler. I've got to get back to taking orders and serving grub." Daisy hugged Tessa again and headed back toward the kitchen. Serena's gaze met Beth's and she couldn't help but read the sadness in the other woman's eyes. Although several months had passed since her husband had gone to prison, Serena couldn't imagine how stressful Beth's life had become, especially having to raise her young daughter alone. Jamie was a bundle of joy, energetic and happy. She seemed to be handling her father's absence better than her mother.

"How are things going with you, Beth? Have you considered moving to Shiloh Springs full time?" The last time Beth had visited Tessa, she'd toyed around with the idea of relocating from North Carolina, making a brand new start away from the memories of her ex-husband and being closer to the only family she had left.

"I was planning to talk to you and Ms. Patti." She took a deep breath. "I've contacted a realtor in North Carolina, and

I'm putting the house up for sale."

Tessa reached over and pulled her sister in close for a hug. "I'm so happy. I swear, you're going to love Shiloh Springs. Plus, you already know practically everybody, so it's not like you're uprooting your life and moving to a town full of strangers." She grinned. "You've got us!" Tessa gestured toward the other women at the table.

"Anything I can help with, you know I'm there." Serena smiled at Beth. "But you seem a little, I don't know...sad this morning. Can I help?"

Beth shook her head. "It's nothing. Well, it's not nothing, but I'm trying not to dwelling on it. I—got a letter from Evan a couple of days ago."

"What? How'd he know you were here?" Outrage tinged Tessa's voice. "I'll call Rafe, and have him talk to the warden. Evan shouldn't be allowed to harass you—"

"Stop! He's not harrassing me. He mailed the letter to the North Carolina address. The Millers have been forwarding everything to me once a week, after tossing out all the junk. The letter was in the stuff I got from them."

Tessa flopped back in her chair, muttering under her breath. Evan Stewart wasn't her favorite person, Serena knew, since the man had tried to kill her when she'd first moved to Shiloh Springs. He'd been trying to steal a county bond, one which had been in Tessa and Beth's family for over a hundred years, and was worth millions. He and his partner-in-crime, who happened to be Tessa's ex-boyfriend, held her hostage until Rafe and his brother rescued her, and put Evan and Trevor behind bars.

"What did he want?"

"Calm down, Rambo. He wanted to know how Jamie was doing without him around. He misses his daughter. I think he wants me to consider bringing her for a visit."

"Uh-uh, no way! You can't possibly be thinking it's a good idea, right?"

"Of course not. I would never take Jamie anywhere near her father, especially with him being locked up. He deserves everything he's going through. He brought it on himself by being such a no-good you-know-what."

Serena watched the interplay between the sisters, saw the love and friendship, the special bond being part of a family shining through, and felt a twinge of guilt. She'd had that once. A family she loved with all her heart, until they'd done something so heinous she'd had to turn her back on them and walk away. But it didn't mean she'd stopped thinking about them, or stopped loving them. She simply couldn't be a part of the life they lived, not and be able to look at herself in the mirror.

"What else did the jerk's letter say?" This from Jill, who'd sat quietly throughout Tessa's diatribe about Evan, his letter, and the blunt instrument Tessa planned to use upside his head if he even hinted about bothering Beth or Jamie again.

"Mostly how sorry he is for everything." She glanced at

Tessa. "He wants to write and tell you personally he's sorry, but he's afraid to, you know, because of Rafe. I think he's afraid of your fiancé."

"He should be," Tessa mumbled.

"It's funny, he spent a lot of time talking about some guy in the SuperMax prison out in Colorado, and how he's this big cheese. It's like he's got a man crush on this dude. Went on and on about how he's got a whole bunch of followers who practically worship the ground he walks on, a lot of his fellow prisoners. Said this guy in Colorado has been meeting with his lawyers a lot recently, although it's all been very hush-hush. From the way he talks, I think he might be one of this guy's newest converts."

Serena's muscles tensed with each word Beth spoke. It couldn't be possible. What were the odds of Beth's ex knowing anything about her uncle? No, she had to be wrong. There were other charismatic prisoners all over the country. Didn't mean the one Evan Stewart was enamored with was Big Jim. They weren't even in the same prison. Evan was in Huntsville and Big Jim was in ADX Florence, one of the most secure prisons in the world.

"Evan said rumors started trickling down through the grapevine this guy, who was apparently nabbed by the feds, is angling for a new trial, and the scuttlebutt amongst the other prisoners is it looks like he's gonna get one."

"His prison grapevine sounds better informed than some of the paparazzi following the stars." Jill tried to lighten the conversation, but Serena's thoughts rolled through her mind at breakneck speed. Evan's letter couldn't possibly mean Big Jim. Her uncle had been convicted, with more than enough evidence to keep him behind bars for eternity.

"Did Evan mention this man's name? The one who's trying to get a new trial?" She tried to keep her tone light, though the clenched hands in her lap belied the calm façade she projected.

"Hang on," Beth said, before digging in her purse. Within a few seconds, she pulled a crumpled envelope out, and waved it like a trophy. "Got it right here. It's...Berkley. James Berkley. Evan called him Big Jim." She scoffed. "Like he knows him personally or something. Not likely, since he's hundreds and hundreds of miles away."

The breakfast Serena had just finished threatened to do a repeat performance, and she closed her eyes, willing her stomach and her mind to calm. This couldn't be happening. She knew she should have listened to her gut the second she saw the stupid picture in the magazine, instead of letting Ms. Patti talk her into staying. She needed to leave, hightail it out of Shiloh Springs before the feds or one of Big Jim's goons tracked her to the real estate office.

"Well, ladies, it's been fun, but I've gotta run." She inwardly winced at her choice of words. "I've got a full day ahead of me." Reaching into her purse, she pulled a twenty out of her wallet and tossed it onto the table, her hands shaking and her mind racing. "I'll see you later."

Tessa and Jill stood and gave her hugs, and she squeezed

them both tight, her heart breaking because she'd probably never see them again. These lovely women had opened their hearts and their lives and become her best friends. Would they understand she was doing what she thought best? If she stuck around, they could all be in danger. While the feds would put her back in witness protection, if Big Jim's men got to her first, they wouldn't care who else might be around. They'd simply look at the women as collateral damage, lives easily discarded and tossed aside, as long as they accomplished their final goal—eliminating her. She stiffened her spine, and looped the handle of her bag over her shoulder.

Maybe someday she'd be able to come back, or let them know why she'd run. But life was filled with maybes and somedays. It was for the best to let them forget her, let her become a fond memory of somebody they once knew. Serena wasn't willing to put their lives, their futures, in jeopardy.

Pausing at the door, she took one last look back at the four women, and silently wished them happy and healthy lives, filled with laughter and friendship and love. All things she knew weren't part of her future. Didn't matter though— it was time to run—again.

Run, as far and as fast as she could. Her only regret was she'd never see Antonio Boudreau again. Her one secret fantasy, the light in her darkness, and he'd never know how she felt about him. Because it was too late, and she had run out of options.

She had to disappear.

CHAPTER FIVE

The alarm buzzed as the steel door swung inward. Big Jim Berkley watched the guard motion his lawyer through the doorway, whispering something to him as he entered. Jonathan Drury appeared pale, his skin carried a sheen of sweat, and he'd bet his palms were clammy to the touch. Nodding vigorously to the guard, Jonathan stepped the rest of the way into the visiting area. Big Jim wasn't worried. It was probably the guard's routine warning to stay on his side of the table, and far away from the dangerous prisoner. Blah, blah, blah. He chuckled. Like he'd do anything to upset the applecart at this stage of the game. Nobody in their right mind was stupid enough to rock the boat when they were trying to get out of this cesspit.

Jonathan Drury, his attorney of record, and one of his most loyal followers, had finally finagled, wheedled, and bribed enough people to get Big Jim a new trial, and he wasn't going to screw around and get himself stuck back into solitary. There was too much to get done if he ever wanted to see daylight again as a free man.

Jonathan slid onto the seat across from him, a bead of

sweat trickling down his forehead and onto his cheek. Big Jim grinned, pleased he still instilled fear in the man. Thus far, the other man had been incompetent, allowing the feds to build a rock solid case against him, though he hadn't been able to figure out who, besides his dear niece, had practically handed him over like a prize pig on a platter complete with an apple in his mouth to the feds. There wasn't a shadow of doubt somebody had flapped their jaws, probably to save their own hide. But find out he would—and they'd pay dearly for betraying him and his cause.

"Do you have news for me?"

Jonathan swallowed, his Adam's apple bobbing with the movement. The gold, wire-rimmed glasses slid down the bridge of his nose, and he pushed them up, his hand trembling slightly, but enough Big Jim could see it. A cold smile touched his lips, and Drury's skin took on a sallow appearance.

"There's no sign of your niece, sir." The nasally whine of Jonathan's voice grated, but he dismissed it, focusing instead on the actual words.

"Nothing? You've had two years to find her. How hard can it be to find one woman with no friends and no family, boy? At least no family that'll help the no-good traitor."

"I—I've got everybody working round-the-clock, trying to find her. The last time anybody saw her was in Lincoln. Since she slipped out of the hospital, she's stayed off the grid. Nobody has used her ID, credit cards, nothing. Not under any name we've got for her."

Big Jim bounded from his chair, and paced back and forth on his side of the table, careful not to give the guard watching his every move a reason to interrupt his alone time with his attorney. He wasn't allowed visitors regularly, and the only way to keep in touch with his followers was through Drury, the little wimp cowering before him. Though he had to admit, ever since he'd been arrested, Drury had come through time and again, stymying all the federal government's attempts to put him away for the rest of his life. Maybe he wasn't a useless sack of skin after all. He'd reserve judgment—for now.

"Has there been any news on the trial date?"

"Umm, I've submitted a motion with the court to have the case expedited. Of course, the Department of Justice isn't happy with me, and wants to delay as much as possible. It's obvious they're hunting for Sharon, too, but they've had even less luck than we have in finding her."

Big Jim focused his gaze on the attorney, watched with satisfaction as the man squirmed in his seat. Oh, how he missed the power he'd held in his hands with his most loyal followers, the ones he'd led like sheep wherever he pointed them. A few carefully chosen words here and there, and they'd worshipped the ground he walked on. He'd have that feeling again, and soon, because nobody was gonna keep him pinned behind bars much longer. One way or another, he'd be a free man.

"Put more men on it. I want answers, and I want them now. Sharon was never the smartest girl, and I doubt much has changed. She'll pop up soon, and when she does, I want you ready. You'd better make sure we get to her before the feds, or it's all over. Do you understand? I can't stomach betrayal, especially by family. We have to make an example of her, so others know they can't get away with disobedience."

"Sir, umm, there might be a problem with that. We're kinda…low on funds. The money left in the one account the feds didn't freeze is almost gone."

Big Jim let loose a bellow loud enough to have the guard swing open the door and step through. "Everything okay in here, Mr. Drury?"

Little piss-ant. Should be asking me, not this sniveling coward.

"Everything's fine. Get out." Big Jim motioned for the guard to close the door when he didn't move fast enough.

"It's okay, Officer. No problems here." Jonathan nodded and pointed to Big Jim. "He was a little upset with the delays in scheduling his new trial."

"Keep it down." The guard closed the door, but Big Jim could see him standing outside, peering through the glass. He rolled his eyes, and brought his attention back to Drury.

"All your accounts are still frozen. We can't touch any of the funds, sir."

Big Jim pulled out the chair and spun it around, straddling it. He steepled his fingers along the back, his lips pursed as he thought. A smile curled his mouth upward, and he chuckled.

"I bet they don't know about the account I set up in the Caymans, do they? The one under Sharon's name? Even she doesn't know about it."

Jonathan visibly perked up, sitting straighter, his eyes shining with delight. "I forgot all about that account. Do you think…could the money still be there after all this time? Surely the government would have found it when they froze all your other assets?"

Big Jim chuckled, and rubbed his hands together. "Nope. The account had only been open a few days when they hauled me in on their trumped-up charges. It wasn't listed with any of my so-called assets. And I certainly didn't tell them about it." He rose, tall and straight, feeling invigorated. "Get out of here and use the money from the Caymans account. I don't care what it takes, get the money and get Sharon."

"Yes, sir. I'll be in touch."

Like a sniveling little cockroach, Drury scuttled out of the room as fast as his scrawny legs carried him, shutting the door behind him, leaving Big Jim alone with his thoughts. Sharon had surprised him. Despite what he'd said to Drury, he didn't underestimate his niece. She'd proven a worthy adversary, and he wouldn't make the same mistakes again. The odds of her being able to stay hidden were slim, regardless of the fact she'd managed to evade his searches thus far. Between the men on the streets his attorney hired, and the hackers his brother-in-law had working behind the scenes, it was only a matter of time before his sweet niece was once again within the fold of her loving family.

Then she'd learn the real cost of betrayal.

CHAPTER SIX

A ntonio juggled his keys, the extra-large coffee, and the copies of the files he'd brought home to work on in one hand, and pushed open the door to his hotel room. He'd planned on driving back to Shiloh Springs after getting his assignment with the Austin office. Instead, he'd been dragged along on a call involving a hostage situation in downtown Austin, and hadn't made it back to the FBI offices until close to ten o'clock. Fortunately, the situation diffused without any casualties, and he'd gotten a feel for the fellow agents in his temporary location. Bunking down in a hotel for the night made more sense than the hour and a half drive back to Shiloh Springs.

Tossing the files onto the bed, he sat on the edge, pulled off his cowboy boots and socks, letting his toes sink into the carpet. He hated wearing shoes, always had. He smiled at the memory of his momma constantly after him to put on some shoes. But there was something about the feel of grass and dirt beneath his feet, the squishy mud between his toes that felt natural. Maybe he'd inherited his free spirit from his biological mother. He didn't have a lot of fond memories from when he was growing up, but he did remember she'd always loved the outdoors and nature. One of his fondest memories of her was the day she'd taken him to the riverbank and let him wade in the rushing water. Icy cold, it caught the breath in the back of his throat, and she'd laughed, splashing beside him, head thrown back and arms spread at her sides, her smiling face lifted to the sunlight. Funny, he hadn't thought about those moments in years.

He'd just picked up the file on Big Jim Berkley when his cell phone rang. Smiling at the picture on the caller ID screen, he answered. "Hey, Brody. What's up?"

"Antonio! Heard you're in Austin for a while. What gives?"

Trying to get comfortable, Antonio moved around until his back rested against the headboard. One thing he disliked about working in hotel rooms—finding a comfortable place to dig in and get comfortable. He missed his apartment in Dallas, where he had everything in its place, and he could hunker down and have everything within easy reach and not have to get up and search for the stuff he needed.

"The FBI office here is short-staffed, so I'm on loan from Dallas. Means I'll be closer to home for a while."

"Any idea how long you'll be sticking around?"

"Not sure. Could be a few weeks to a few months, depending on the work load outta Austin, and how long it takes to solve the case they've assigned me."

Brody laughed. "They've already stuck you with a case?

Guess they saw the word *sucker* written across your forehead and gave you the worst assignment they had, right?"

"Jackass." Antonio was used to his brother's ribbing. There'd been an on-again, off-again rivalry between them for years, but he knew when the chips were down, Brody had his back. No questions asked. That was the thing about all the Boudreaus. While they might not share blood, their bond was unbreakable and permanent. He couldn't imagine not having all of them in his life, even though the cost of belonging to their family came at a high price.

"You plan on finding a place in Austin while you're there, or commute back and forth to Shiloh Springs?"

"Not sure yet. I've got a hotel room for the next night or two, until I get my feet planted, then we'll see. I kinda want to get a feel for how this office operates, the similarities and differences between here and Dallas. Figure out the movers and shakers, and who the wannabes are too."

"So, you're in Austin right now?"

Antonio heard something in Brody's voice, though he couldn't put his finger on what might have his big brother on edge. "Yeah, like I said, I've got a room."

"Awesome. Which hotel?"

Antonio rattled off the name and room number, wondering what mischief his brother was contemplating. Working out of Dallas kept him away from Shiloh Springs more than he wanted. While it was only a few hours' drive, he didn't get home nearly as often as he'd like, and he'd kinda fallen out of touch with what was happening with his brothers. He'd have to change that.

"I'll pick you up in ten minutes."

"Wait, what? You're here?"

"Yep," Brody chuckled. "Forty-eight hours off shift. Decided I needed to throw caution to the wind and howl at the moon. Since you're here too, I'm taking you with me."

Now Antonio was convinced something was bugging his big brother. Brody wanting to go out on the town and get wild and rowdy? Nope. No way. He was *Captain America*, never stepping a foot over the line of right and wrong. Rarely drank more than a beer, and those were few and far between. Might be a good idea to meet up, see if he could help with whatever troubled his big brother.

"I'll be waiting."

Hanging up, he loosened the tie around his neck and tossed it onto the bed, next to the jacket he abandoned the minute he'd hit the room. Grabbing a pair of jeans and a T-shirt from his suitcase, he quickly changed, splashed water on his face, and brushed his teeth. When a loud knock sounded, he slid his wallet in his pocket and opened the door.

"Brody. Good to see you." He wrapped his arms around his brother, doing the masculine hug and pound on the back greeting all guys did. Stepping back, he studied the man before him. Brody looked pretty much the same as the last time he'd seen him a couple of months earlier. Tall and muscular, his sandy-brown hair was a little longer than it had been. Though he smiled, there was a haunted look in his brilliant blue eyes belying his jovial attitude.

Last time Antonio had been in Shiloh Springs for a quick visit, he'd ended up helping Rafe and an ex-Navy SEAL, Dylan Roberts, protect a woman from a potential stalker kidnapper, who wanted to take her baby out of the country. Maybe Brody was a little thinner, but otherwise there wasn't any outward appearance something bothered his brother. Except his haunted eyes.

"Ready to go?" Brody glanced around Antonio's room, his eyes landing on the files. He bumped his shoulder against Antonio's in a playful manner, before heading toward the bed. "Already bringing work home with you, I see."

Antonio reached past him and grabbed the files, stuffed them into his suitcase and locked it. Pretty dumb, leaving them lying around a hotel room in plain sight. He really needed to get his head in the game, or he'd make mistakes. And mistakes got people killed.

"I don't want to think about work tonight. Plenty of time for that later. Where are we headed?"

"Someplace with lots of music, lots of lovely ladies, and an abundance of booze."

"In Austin? Shouldn't be hard to find." Antonio grinned. Austin's unofficial motto was *Keep Austin Weird*. The entire city was eclectic and having a good time and partying kept the whole place thriving. "You want to grab some food first?"

Brody shrugged. "I could eat."

"Is our food truck stand still here? I could use a couple of those tacos we had the last time we came to Austin."

"Sounds good. I've got my car, I'll drive."

The food truck courtyard bustled with activity, bodies milling around. Boisterous laughter filled the air, along with live music from the band on the far side of the courtyard. The bases of the trees interspersed throughout the gathering place were rimmed with Christmas lights, while additional strands crisscrossed overhead, between the lampposts surrounding the courtyard, like a canopy of stars overhead. Maneuvering through the throng of bodies took skill and determination, but Antonio eventually made it to the taco truck he'd targeted. His mouth watered at the smell of the freshly-cooked beef and spices emanating through the open window of the festively painted food truck, where a pretty Hispanic girl passed out plastic baskets overflowing with Tex-Mex goodness.

"Hey, bro, what do you want? My treat." Antonio stood behind a customer, next in line to place his order. Brody scanned the hand-lettered sign beside the truck's open window, the available items and prices listed. While there weren't a lot of items listed, this truck was a personal favorite of Antonio's, and he'd tried pretty much everything they offered, and knew the menu by heart.

"Grab me a couple of the brisket tacos and a chicken one. Extra guacamole."

Antonio moved forward, placing their order to the smiling girl, who relayed it to the two burly men cooking on the flattops. With a quick efficiency belying their sizes, the men worked with tag-team efficiency and skill. Within minutes, he had two red plastic baskets, overflowing with tasty Tex-Mex food. The intoxicating smell had his taste buds salivating and his stomach growling. He hadn't taken time for a lunch break with the whole hostage situation that afternoon, and his empty belly let him know it was past time to fill up with something hearty and delicious.

Brody snagged them a couple of beers and a table with two empty seats, far enough away from the musicians they'd be able to talk without yelling. Dropping onto the folding chair, he handed Brody his food and picked up a brisket taco, taking a huge bite. The spices hit first, with the smoky beef and cool *pico de gallo*. He almost moaned when the taste of tomato, onion, and cilantro exploded on his taste buds. Before he knew it, he'd demolished the first taco in three bites.

"Geez, man, didn't you eat today?"

Antonio shook his head, picking up the chicken taco next. "Had to deal with a crisis, worked straight through the afternoon. Other than coffee, this is the first thing I've eaten today."

"That's rough. So, what're your thoughts about working in Austin?"

Antonio grabbed a napkin and wiped his mouth before answering. "It's different. Than Dallas, I mean. I get the feeling while they're just as busy, there's a quieter vibe. Know what I mean? Although this afternoon had everybody scrambling, hitting the streets en masse. Hostage situation downtown. You'll probably hear about it on the news, if you haven't already."

Brody nodded. "Caught a bit about it on the radio, driving here. Sounded serious."

"It's always serious when kids are involved." Antonio took a long pull of his beer. "Some people don't deserve to have children." He regretted his words almost immediately when a haunted expression crossed Brody's face. Son of a gun, he'd stuck his foot in his mouth again, spoke without thinking. Not in a million years would he want to hurt his brother. Brody never talked about his biological parents. As far as he knew, he hadn't talked to any of his brothers about what his life was like before he'd become a Boudreau, and Douglas and Ms. Patti never talked about what brought any of the boys to their home and into their lives. Not unless they'd discussed it with each of them first. He had a good idea of some of the stuff Brody endured in his early years. They'd shared a room at The Big House when Antonio had first come to live there. Brody's nightmares were his own business, though Antonio would be there if he ever wanted to talk.

"Y'all got the mom and kids out safe, right?" Brody leaned back in his chair, hands crossed over his midsection. "They mentioned something about a daycare center?"

"Yeah. Messy divorce. Wife got custody of all three kids. The ex followed her to the daycare center, and tried to get the kids to leave with him. Fortunately, the staff alerted us right away. The majority of the kids were out back playing and out of the line of fire."

"Good. Kids need to be protected from the bad stuff. Emotional trauma sticks around for a long time."

"At least the father's behind bars now, and after this stunt, he'll be there for a long time. Endangering not only his own kids, but the others at the daycare—judge will probably throw the book at him. Unless his lawyer goes for diminished capacity, then it'll be up to the lawyers and the shrinks to sort it out."

Brody picked up his bottle and began picking at the label, before taking another drink. "So, you said they've already assigned you a case. Anything you can talk about?"

"Generalities only. Can't give you any details. A woman testified in a case and went into witness protection. Something happened to spook her, and she's disappeared. No one can find her."

Brody's gaze met his. "Not necessarily a bad thing. Witness protection means she had to be protected by being given a new identity and a new place to live. Maybe whatever scared her caused her to do the same thing, only on her own, without telling the government why she was running."

"But it also means nobody is there to protect her if the bad guys come after her. She doesn't have anybody to turn to for help."

Brody placed his beer back on the table and leaned forward, resting his elbows on the edge of the table. "If she ran, she's probably scared of something—or somebody—coming after her. Could whoever she testified against have found her, despite witness protection? Nothing against the feds doing their jobs, but sometimes no matter how hard you work, somebody's always smarter, faster, or more determined to get the job done."

Antonio sighed. "That's what I'm thinking. I don't have all the details yet, but from what I've read in the file, and what the SAC relayed, somebody tried to take her out. Neighbor was killed and she basically ghosted. When she resurfaced, she was in a different city, different state, and contacted WITSEC. She was given another new identity, new job, new city."

Brody grimaced. "Lemme guess, somehow they found her again." Antonio nodded, and Brody continued. "Sounds like there's a leak in your witness protection program."

"There was. I've been told the leak has been effectively plugged."

"But not quick enough to save your girl, right?"

"She's alive, though she was hurt. At least, we think she's still alive."

Brody picked up his bottle and toasted, "Good for her. I bet she didn't contact the feds again, and struck out on her own, right?"

"Pretty much. Now I have to find her."

Brody studied him. "Why? Seems like the witness protection folks failed her not once, but twice. I figure it's pretty smart for her not to trust anybody else with her safety at this point. It's what I'd do, if I was in her shoes."

Antonio scrubbed his hand along his jaw. "If only it were that simple. Unfortunately, the guy she testified against is getting a new trial. Without her testimony, chances are good he'll walk. Trust me, bro, you do not want this guy walking the streets a free man. Look up the word evil in the dictionary and his picture would be there."

"You think she knows? About the appeal?"

Antonio shook his head, studying his brother's face. "I doubt it, not unless she's got a connection within the feds. It hasn't been released to the news outlets, but he's getting a new trial. It's being kept quiet for obvious reasons. It would be a social media circus. I've got my work cut out for me piecing together whatever clues I've got to try and find this woman."

"Good luck. I sincerely mean it, although I gotta say, I sympathize with this anonymous chick. She does the right thing, helps put away a seriously bad dude from what you're telling me, and she's done nothing but pay the price since. If I was her, I'd dig the deepest hole I could, and not climb out again. Or better yet, I'd leave the country. Doubt you'd find me then."

"Brody, don't even think it. If she's left the country, I'll never get her to come back to testify."

"Like I said, good luck." Brody stood and picked up the empty food baskets and the two bottles and handed them back to the girl at the food truck. Another thing he liked about Austin, they were big on recycling. He smiled as she put the bottles into a large can marked Glass/Recycle.

He stood when Brody walked back up to the table.

"Ready to hit the town, bro?"

As much as he wanted to head back to the hotel and dig into the files on Big Jim Berkley and his niece, he knew his brother needed this—needed him. To let loose and leave his personal demons behind for a few hours. He'd be there to watch his back—always. It might also give him some insight into what had turned his fun-loving, straight arrow brother into a haunted, closed down stranger since the last time he'd seen him.

"Let's party."

CHAPTER SEVEN

The sun had played peek-a-boo behind the clouds most of the day, and the temperature had dropped several degrees by the time Serena pulled into her parking space. Those same clouds steadily got darker and darker, and with a twinge of a headache beginning behind her eyes, she felt pretty confident it would rain before nightfall.

Staring through the windshield, she studied her home. She loved her townhouse with its two-story charm. In a fortunate turn of events, she'd been able to snag an end unit, when the couple buying it decided to cancel the contract, and she'd snatched it up at a good price. Her fake identification had held up under scrutiny, and the sale had sailed through without a hitch. Though she did wonder if she was making a huge mistake, because chances were good she'd end up on the run again, and leave it all behind. Still, she adored her little corner of Shiloh Springs, carving out a nest where she felt safe laying her head at night.

A combination of wood and brick, it had a modern yet homey appearance which attracted her from the moment she'd seen it. The only drawback, as far as she was concerned at moments like this, was its lack of a garage. Hopefully she'd get everything inside before it started raining, because she was like a cat, and hated to get wet. More than once when she'd been running, hiding from her family and from the feds, she'd spent nights huddled under overhangs with the rain pouring down, cold, soggy and alone. A feeling she hoped she'd never deal with again. She felt strangely *simpatico* with stray animals, because she'd lived enough on the streets to be miserable, and she'd never forgotten the feeling.

Hitting the trunk key on her fob, she quickly unloaded all the grocery bags, along with her garment bag from the dry cleaners, and headed toward the front door. An eerie feeling permeated the air, and Serena froze, furtively looking around, scanning right and left before shaking her head.

You've got to stop this. Nobody knows where you are. You're safe for now.

Unlocking the door, she flicked on the light in the entryway and headed toward the kitchen. Placing the grocery bags on the island, she tossed her purse and keys there too, and she took a steading breath. Ever since the stupid photo showed up in the magazine, she'd found herself constantly looking over her shoulder, flinching at the slightest sound. As hard as she tried to remind herself she was safe, some sixth sense insisted her uncle would find her. Thinking about having to flee again, leave behind everything and everyone in Shiloh Springs, made her breath catch in her chest.

Digging through the grocery sacks, she put away the perishables, especially the pint of chocolate raspberry chip ice cream she intended to savor after dinner. It had been a rough few days and she deserved to reward herself with her favorite treat. She made quick work of putting away the rest of her food, and headed for the living room. Kicking off her heels, she smiled at the coolness of the wooden floor beneath her toes. Was there a better feeling in the world than coming home and kicking off your shoes at the end of the day?

Plopping down on the sofa, she lifted her feet to place them on the coffee table and froze for several excruciatingly long seconds, before lowering them slowly back to the floor. Something wasn't right. The small tray she left on the coffee table to hold the remotes wasn't where she left it. Before it was in the center of the table, yet now it was off to the left by several inches. She replayed in her mind when she'd left her place earlier. Had she somehow moved it, or maybe hit the table in passing? The small potted African violet wasn't in its usual place, either.

Rising from the sofa, she moved around the living room, studying every angle, every item. The differences were subtle, but they were there. Little things out of place. She'd be the first to admit she was a tad OCD about where things belonged. Things needed to be symmetric, and everything had its proper place, and now they weren't where she'd left them. Nothing big or obvious, but definitely not how she'd left her place earlier, she was positive.

Taking tentative steps down the hall, she glanced into the guest room. Yep, it was the same in there. Though the room was sparsely decorated, because she rarely used it, little things were off-kilter or out of place from where they belonged. Her hands felt clammy, and she wiped them along her slacks before clenching them into fists. The sick feeling in the pit of her stomach grew, and she fought the bile rising in the back of her throat.

Finally, she made her way to her bedroom and swung open the door. At first glance, everything looked exactly like she'd left it earlier. The bed was made with its dark turquoise bedspread. Accent pillows of turquoise and burnt orange and white decorated the top, precisely the way she'd placed them. The nightstands on either side of the bed held silver-based lamps with white shades, each centered in place. Nothing out of place there, either.

Finally, her gaze landed on the dresser, and she swallowed back her scream. The top drawer on the right wasn't closed all the way, and the strap from one of her bras was caught on the edge. She definitely hadn't left it like that when she'd gotten dressed. Reaching for it, she stopped herself from touching it at the last second. There might be fingerprints left behind by whoever had been here. Deep in her gut, she knew what this meant.

Someone had been in her home. Searched her place. Touched her things. She wrapped her arms around her middle, and fell to her knees at the thought, because it could only mean one thing.

They'd found her.

Antonio pulled up in front of the sheriff's station and killed the engine. He'd spent the better part of the morning and early afternoon going over the files SAC Williamson gave him. After spending most of the night with Brody until the wee hours, he wasn't any closer to figuring out what ate at his brother, though he wasn't about to give up. As long as he stayed in Shiloh Springs, he planned on doing a little digging into Brody's problem, because he couldn't stand to see his brother hurting. Whatever it took, he'd find a way to make things better. Because that's what family did.

He still had a hard time wrapping his head around what he'd discovered in the Berkley files. Big Jim's case was pretty straightforward. He was a thug and a terrorist with delusions of grandeur. The world was lucky he'd been caught and thrown behind bars before somebody was seriously hurt or killed. He'd been escalating his attacks, and it was only a matter of time before the inevitable happened. The only surprise was the feds hadn't caught the bully sooner. But it was the other file, the one on Sharon Berkley, throwing him for a loop.

The second he'd opened the file and looked at the picture of Sharon Berkley, the bottom dropped out of his world. Recognition flared instantly. She'd changed her hair color. Changed the style. Even the color of her eyes was different, easy enough nowadays with colored contact lenses. But there was no disguising that face. The face he saw every night when he closed his eyes.

His Serena.

The woman who'd moved to Shiloh Springs. Made herself part of the community. Part of his family. There was no disputing the facts—Serena Snowden was Sharon Berkley, the woman being hunted by WITSEC, the FBI, and countless others. If he was to hazard a guess, Big Jim Berkley probably had a passel of hired goons searching for her too. She was the key who could bring Big Jim's kingdom tumbling down around him once and for all.

A rap on his window broke him from his thoughts, and he stared at the man standing outside his door. His brother, Rafe, leaned downward, with a smile on his face. He motioned for his brother to get in the car. Once seated, Rafe swiveled to face his brother.

"What's up?"

Antonio drew in a deep breath before answering. "We need to talk."

"Okay. Business or family?"

He knew exactly what his brother meant. If it was business, Rafe would do what he could within the limits of the law to help. Being in law enforcement himself, Antonio understood and appreciated his brother's stance. If the problem was family, there were no boundaries to what Rafe would do. All the Boudreau brothers had an ingrained sense of right and wrong, taught from the moment they stepped through the doors at the Big House, the Boudreau family homestead. Loyalty, honesty, integrity—traits lovingly taught by Douglas and Ms. Patti. These things became embedded into the lives of each Boudreau. Wasn't to say a few of the boys who passed through their home didn't make it. Sometimes the foster system failed, no matter how hard those working to give a helping hand tried. Circumstances couldn't always be overcome, and sometimes, no matter how hard everyone worked, people had free will and made wrong choices. Then it was up to them to pay the consequences of the choices made.

The one thing they'd been taught, from the moment they walked through the doorway until they left, was family came first. No matter what, family always helped family. In times of need, family stepped up, no questions asked, and did whatever it took to help out a brother in need.

He pondered his answer for a long moment. "Business. Family. I don't know—both maybe?"

"Wanna go inside and talk?"

Antonio shook his head. The more he thought about it, he realized he didn't want an official investigation on the part of Shiloh Springs Sheriff's Department. The FBI was already going to have problems with him handling this case, probably be screaming bloody murder about conflict of interest, since he knew Serena—Sharon—personally. He'd come to get his brother's opinion, off the record, because he honestly wasn't sure what to do. As an FBI agent, he knew his job. Knew he should head straight for Serena's place, and take her into custody for her own protection. As a man, he wanted to do the same, protect her and keep her safe from everybody, which included Big Jim and the government. He knew he didn't have his head on straight, and needed a second unbiased opinion. An added bonus, he knew Rafe could keep his mouth shut.

"Can you take a break? I've got a case I'd like to get your opinion on, but it's a bit…sensitive."

Rafe eyeballed him, and Antonio met his gaze straight on. Finally, Rafe nodded his head and opened the car door.

"Give me a second to let Sally Anne where I'll be. Be right back."

A couple minutes later, Rafe slid onto the passenger seat again. "Unless there's an emergency, I'm yours for the rest of the afternoon. Now do you want to tell me what's got you wrapped up so tight you're about to bust?"

Reaching beside his seat, Antonio pulled out the file on Big Jim Berkley, and tossed it to Rafe. When his brother simply held the file and quirked a brow, Antonio laughed. His brother understood him so well.

"Caught a case out of the Austin office. You know I'm helping cover down there for a few weeks, while they're short-staffed, right?" At Rafe's nod, he started the engine and pulled onto the street. "The SAC hit me with this yesterday. You might remember the case. Big Jim Berkley?"

"Yeah, I remember it. Guy liked to bomb places like synagogues and mosques, right? Didn't they arrest him? I thought he went away for life plus something like three hundred years."

"Well, bro, off the record, it looks like his attorneys got him a new trial."

Rafe let loose a string of curses. "He's as dirty as they come. I remember following a good chunk of the trial, but kinda lost track after he was convicted. How could they possibly justify giving him another trial?"

"He's either got a very good lawyer or somebody's on the take. Maybe both. It's not common knowledge yet. The feds are keeping mum, because there's a catch."

Rafe looked up from the pages he'd started flipping through. "There's always a catch, isn't there?"

"Remember the niece? The one who testified against him and a bunch of her family members during the trial? She's the one who turned them in in the first place."

"I remember her." Rafe tapped the folder against his knee, staring out the windshield. "Didn't she go into witness protection afterward? Big Jim made some not-so-veiled threats in open court about how she'd pay for her treachery and betraying the family."

"Uh-huh. There's the rub. Sharon Berkley is in the wind."

"Can't be good for the feds' case. I seem to remember she was pretty much the lynchpin holding their case together. Can't they use her previous testimony against him?"

"Not as long as she's still alive, they can't. What is it they always say, the accused has the right to face his accuser? If she's not there to testify, the government's case is pretty much circumstantial evidence, and from what I've been told, shaky at best. Without Sharon Berkley's testimony, chances are good he'll walk."

"How do you play into all of this?"

"The case I've been handed is to find Sharon Berkley."

Rafe barked a laugh. "Kind of a tall order for one man, isn't it? I'd think on a case this big, they'd have scores of agents looking for her."

"They do, spread out all over the country. I happened to luck into the local case because the agent they'd assigned had appendicitis and had to be rushed to surgery."

"Tough luck."

They drove for a few minutes in silence, and Antonio pulled over and parked in the parking lot of the elementary school, and watched his brother's eye scan the building. He knew exactly where Rafe's mind had gone, straight to his fiancée, Tessa. He hadn't been thinking about that when he'd pulled in here, he'd simply wanted to stop for a few minutes to hash out the case with Rafe, because he was about to drop the big bombshell.

He opened his mouth, but before he could say anything,

Rafe's cell phone rang. Glancing at the caller ID, Rafe shrugged and murmured "sorry" before answering.

"Hello." There was a warmth in his voice, which immediately told Antonio it was somebody Rafe knew and cared about on the other end of the phone. "No, don't touch anything. Lock the doors, and we'll be right over."

"Trouble?"

Rafe nodded. "Maybe. Looks like there might be a break-in. I need you to drive."

"No problem. Where to?"

Rafe's gaze met his. "Serena's place."

CHAPTER EIGHT

Something big was in the air. Big Jim could practically taste it. Like anticipation of something just out of reach, a prized toy dangling beyond his fingertips. If he reached for it too soon, somebody would snatch it away. But he could wait. He'd learned to be infinitely patient since being locked behind these walls. Not for much longer, though. Freedom hovered just beyond his grasp, growing closer each day, tantalizing him with the possibilities awaiting him when he walked out a free man, with the world at his feet.

The long stretch of hallway taunted him, the stretch from his cell like an endless tunnel, the putrid color an affront to his senses, and he stumbled, grabbing onto the wall to steady his balance. The muffled chuckle from the guard stabbed at him, mocking him at the overwhelming sense of powerlessness of being incarcerated in this stinking hole in Colorado. As much as he hated the chains they slapped on him every time he had to walk the dank, dreary halls to meet with his lawyer, he smirked at the thought one day they'd come off for the last time. Never again would he breathe the fetid stench of confinement behind prison walls.

He yearned to feel sunlight on his face, drink in the luxury of going where he pleased, answerable to no one but himself.

Drury better have good news this time. He was tired of nothing but failures with each visit. Everything depended on finding his niece. Her ingenuity at outwitting the lackwits in witness protection still amused him. It also infuriated him, because she'd become the elusive prize hindering his every move. The MacGuffin in his Hitchcock drama, but not for much longer.

Sitting in the hard chair, he remained still as the guard took off his shackles. Physical encounters with the guards resulted in nothing more than solitary confinement and punishments for what they alleged was bad behavior. The lily-livered wimps didn't know the meaning of the term. He'd played nice thus far. If only they knew what he had in store for them once he was free, they'd cower from him in abject terror.

It was another couple of minutes before Drury came through the doorway. Face flushed, he looked both excited and terrified. He came in empty-handed. The prison rules stated he couldn't bring in his briefcase or even a cell phone, nothing the prisoner might take. Little did the guards know, things like phones, drugs, and other illegal items could be easily obtained inside their hallowed walls if the price was right. Sometimes he wondered at the naiveté of the United States judicial system. Wondered at it, but utilized it to his advantage.

"Sir, I wish I had better news."

Definitely wasn't the start of the conversation Big Jim had anticipated. No, he'd been certain Drury would come bearing good news this time, not the same old nothing. His hands clenched into fists beneath the table, and he breathed deeply, struggling to regain his composure. The guard stood right outside the door, glaring through the glass panel, waiting for him to make the slightest mistake. This guard in particular always seemed to delight in tormenting him. Chuck something or other. He'd make sure Chuck and his family became one of the first to feel his wrath, once he was free again.

"Spit it out, Drury."

"We've done everything we can to access the account in the Cayman Islands, the one under Sharon's name. We can't touch it."

He gritted his teeth. Dealing with incompetents put him in a really bad mood. "Why?"

"The bank, located on Grand Cayman, won't release any funds without Sharon Berkley being present in person. The bank president stated the way the account was set up, the account requires in-person access only."

"Impossible." He leaned forward, eyes narrowed. "What moron thought that was a good idea? I certainly didn't authorize it." Drawing in a calming breath, Big Jim leaned back in the chair and struggled to maintain control. He was so tired of dealing with other people's stupidity. "Have one of the hackers get into account, and transfer the money to another. Create a new one the feds don't know about. It's not rocket science."

Drury fumbled with the knot of his tie, his breath coming faster, face bright red. At the visible shaking of his hands, Big Jim leaned back in his chair. If he intimated the little weasel too much, Drury might have a heart attack, and then he'd be back to square one. No, he was too close to getting it all to screw up now.

"The…the hackers can't get in. There's some kind of new software the bank instituted to prevent fraudulent access. They're working on it, I swear! I…I don't understand how the account got set up for in-person access only."

Big Jim tapped his fingertips against the tabletop, trying to think back to when the account was created. It happened right before the feds arrested him. He kept a tight rein on the flow of funds, incoming and outgoing. Money was power, and he craved power like a politician craved popularity. Nobody pulled a fast one on him and lived to tell about it. Nobody. Nothing had been done differently he could remember. His brother-in-law transferred the money to a brand new account in the Caymans. Could he have screwed things up? Too bad he wasn't around to ask him.

"Abner was the last person to touch the account. If it's screwed up, he's the one. We gotta get somebody down to Grand Cayman with fake ID, pretending to be Sharon, and get access those funds."

"Umm, I…we already tried. I had my wife…she put on a wig and contacts, and had fake ID…passport, driver's license. They wouldn't—"

"Idiot! Your wife couldn't pass for Sharon. Even a blind man could tell they aren't the same person. She's gotta be what, seventy-five to a hundred pounds bigger? Of course it didn't work."

"It should have. I mean…how would the bank even know what Sharon looks like?"

Big Jim closed his eyes and prayed for patience. They needed to deliver him from having to work with stupid people, because that's all he seemed to be surrounded with these days. He didn't understand Drury's incompetence. In the courtroom, the man was a shark who rarely lost a case. He intimidated opposing counsel on a routine basis with his knowledge and preparedness. But whenever he got around Big Jim, he cowered like a little mouse, afraid of his own shadow.

"All anybody had to do was do a quick Google search. Sharon's pictures are all over the internet from the trial, moron."

"Oh. I didn't think about that. Sorry." Drury hung his head, but then shot up out of his chair. "But, I do have some good news—I think." He shoved a hand into his pocket and pulled out what looked like pages from a magazine. They were wadded up and wrinkled, and he shoved then toward Big Jim.

"What's this?"

"You know my wife gets all those fancy magazines, right?" Drury's voice was laced with excitement. "Stacks and stacks of them, they arrive in the mail all month long. Anyway, she was looking through this magazine and showed me this."

Big Jim smoothed the creases out of the paper before looking at the glossy pages in his hand. The thud of his heartbeat sounded loud in his ears, racing, thumping faster and faster. He blinked twice to make sure his eyes weren't deceiving him, because the picture in his hand looked like—Sharon. His niece. The traitorous witch who'd sold him out to the feds. The woman who'd made his life a living nightmare for the last several years.

"Where is she?"

"It's her, right? I mean…she looks different. The hair's a different color, and you can only see part of her face, but I swear it's her."

Big Jim slowly rose from his chair. "I asked where she is?"

Drury gulped. "Texas." At Big Jim's silent stare, he continued. "A small town called Shiloh Springs…looks like she's working in real estate…if it's her. I had one of your men search her place. He's a pro, so he didn't leave any evidence behind he'd even been there. He's good, I swear! He didn't find anything to prove it's her, but—"

A slow smile spread across Big Jim's lips. "It's her."

Drury slumped into the chair he'd vacated, placing his hands on the table. "What do you…want me…us…to do, boss?"

Big Jim closed his eyes, and allowed the feeling of euphoria to spread throughout him. Finally, after all these months of dreaming about getting the duplicitous, backstabbing witch back in his orbit, he had her.

"Find her—and kill her."

CHAPTER NINE

Antonio pulled into a parking space a few slots down from Serena's townhouse, and slammed on the brakes. Rafe hadn't said another word after taking the call, not even when Antonio exceeded the speed limit—by a lot. Which told him whatever was happening, it was serious.

Rafe flung open the passenger door the second the car rocked to a stop, with Antonio seconds behind. Before they reached the townhouse's front door, it was flung open, Serena highlighted in the opening. Her paleness made him want to pull her into his arms, shelter her from whatever'd caused her distress.

"You gonna let me in, Serena?" Rafe gently touched her arm, and Serena started, her eyes wide with fright.

"I—sorry, come in." She stepped back, allowing them inside. Rafe immediately began looking around the living room, though Antonio wasn't sure exactly what he was searching for. Serena stood there, her arms wrapped around her midsection, a slight hitch in her breathing the only indication of her nervousness. Something had spooked her, though he didn't have a clue what it might have been.

"Talk me through what happened." Rafe's voice when he spoke was soft, filled with concern. "What makes you think somebody's been in your home?"

Antonio stiffened at his brother's words. He'd forgotten Rafe mentioned something about a possible break-in when he'd gotten the phone call. *Somebody had been here? This was Serena's home. Her safe place.* "Somebody's been here?"

Rafe shot him a look, telling him without words to shut his pie hole. Antonio raised his hands, telling his brother he'd gotten the message. This was Rafe's job, his jurisdiction, and he'd play along. *For now.*

"I met with Tessa, Jill, and Beth earlier. Had a girls' morning at Daisy's place. Then I ran a few errands. Picked up some groceries, general chore stuff. I didn't notice anything amiss until I sat down and put my feet up." She pointed to the coffee table. "Things were out of place. Here and here." She touched the tray with the remotes and a small plant.

"How do you know they'd been moved?"

Serena gave a shaky laugh. "I tend to be a little—okay, a lot—OCD at times. I line things up so they're symmetrical or centered. These were right where they were supposed to be this morning, but now they're not. Am I making sense?"

Rafe nodded. "Is there anything else out of place?"

Serena stood, and motioned down the hall. "I didn't check the guest room in depth, but a few things are out of place in there, too. But, in my bedroom—" she broke off speaking and closed her eyes, drawing in another shaky breath.

"Show me, please."

Antonio couldn't help noticing how well his brother handled Serena. He treated her with kid gloves, making her feel safe and taking her concerns seriously. His brother was darned good at his job. It was tough keeping his mouth shut, especially after what he'd discovered about Serena's alter ego. He was sure things could and would be discussed once Rafe figured out what was going on. He'd started to tell Rafe anyway before they'd been interrupted, because A) he was the county sheriff and doing his job, and B) it might be related to what he'd found out about Big Jim's case.

He followed close behind Rafe and Serena, his gaze focused on her. He knew she had a backbone of steel most of the time, but this invasion of her home definitely had her spooked, though she was doing a good job of trying to hide the fact. Stopping in the doorway of her bedroom, he couldn't help looking around. He fantasized about being in Serena's room, though under distinctly different circumstances.

The room itself was big enough for a king-sized bed, covered with a dark turquoise spread. Accent pillows adorned the top. He'd never understood the need women had for adding so many frou-frou pillows on their bed. They always ended up on the floor when you climbed in bed anyway. Seemed like a waste, but at least the ones she'd chosen were nice. Silver lamps sat atop nightstands on either side of the bed. The headboard and footboard were white, which gave the room a beachy feel. It wasn't what he'd pictured for her, yet somehow it fit her personality.

"At first, I didn't notice anything, not like in the other rooms. Not until I saw this." She pointed to the bra strap caught on the drawer. "I definitely didn't leave it like that this morning." Again she wrapped her arms around her midsection, and Antonio fought the urge to pull her close and wrap his own arms around her. "I made sure not to touch anything, once I realized somebody had been here. In case you wanted to check for fingerprints or whatever."

"Exactly what we're going to do, Serena." Rafe pulled out his cell, then met Antonio's gaze. "Why don't you two go back to the living room while I call my team to come and take a look?"

"Come on, sweetheart, let's do what Rafe says. The faster the techs get here, the faster we'll figure out who did this." Antonio gave his brother a brisk nod, and placed his hand on the small of Serena's back, gently steering her back to the living room. With the light touch, he could feel her body trembling beneath his hand, belying the calm exterior she tried to project.

"Okay."

He eased her down onto the sofa, and sat beside her, taking her hands between his. They felt icy cold, and he gently rubbed them, holding them until he felt the warmth return.

"Do you have any idea who might have gotten into your place?"

She shook her head, her eyes locked onto the floor. It was funny how she'd barely looked at him since they'd gotten here, which seemed kinda odd. They were friends—at least he thought they were, even though he'd wanted more. Until he'd seen her picture in that stupid FBI file. Now everything was topsy-turvy and he didn't know up from down, because the woman he knew, the Serena Snowden who'd come to Shiloh Springs a little less than a year ago, was the complete opposite of Sharon Berkley. Didn't matter; he had a job to do, an oath he had to fulfil, which meant turning Sharon Berkley, aka Serena Snowden, over to the feds. Bet SAC Williamson never expected to get results this fast, he mused.

Before he could ask anything else, a loud knock sounded on the door of the townhouse. Serena's body jerked at the sound, and he took her hand in his again. He heard Rafe's heavy tread against the hardwoods, and knew he'd get the door.

"Don't worry. It's just the tech guys, here to do their thing. Get fingerprints, gather evidence. You know, all the stuff you see on television."

Serena gave a shaky laugh. "You always said the stuff they show on television is complete garbage. Nobody does things the way Hollywood portrays it."

"True. But they do need to make sure they double check everything, see if whoever was here left behind anything we might give us an idea who it was. Maybe fibers from clothing, fingerprints, or DNA evidence. It shouldn't take long." He ran his hand along her cheek. Her skin felt like the finest silk beneath his touch. "Can I get you anything? Something to drink maybe?"

She struggled to stand, but he stopped her with a touch. "I should—"

"You stay here and let me take care of you, okay? I'm pretty sure I know where the kitchen is and can find the glasses."

She smiled, finally meeting his gaze. "Thank you."

He paused long enough to watch Rafe direct Dusty and Judith, both from the sheriff's office, toward Serena's bedroom, before heading to the kitchen and getting Serena a drink. Her kitchen was beautiful with bright white cabinetry and quartz countertops. It looked modern, like something out of a magazine, and the complete opposite of what he'd expect Serena to like. Oh, he got it she'd want modern amenities, what woman didn't? He remembered his mother and sister going on and on about tiles, granite, and back-splashes until he'd been ready to pull his hair out when they'd redone the kitchen at the Big House, but somehow this kitchen didn't suit his Serena. It seemed too—stark, almost sterile. There were no personal touches. No cook-books, no appliances. Not even a potted plant graced the pristine countertops.

Walking back into the living room, he handed the water to Serena and glanced around the space. Here, too, he noted a lack of personal touches. Even though she'd been in Shiloh Springs almost a year, there were no photographs, no knick-knacks. Nothing to make it a home, which made him realize she probably didn't consider it a home. Simply another stop on her run away from Big Jim. He bet if he looked in her closet, he'd find a bag packed and ready to go at a moment's notice.

"I think it's a good idea if you come and stay at the Big House for a few days."

Serena's head whipped toward him, eyes wide. "What?"

"Somebody's been in your home. It isn't safe for you to be here alone."

"Antonio, I can't just up and leave my house because somebody broke in. They didn't steal anything. I'll—I'll change the locks. Everything's going to be fine. I overreacted. Maybe nobody's been here and I—"

"You know better. Until we know who got into your place, we need to make sure you're safe." He paused before adding softly, "I need to be sure you're safe."

Serena's gaze searched his, before she finally looked away, and he read the uncertainty in her face. "It seems a little extreme to put everybody out because I might—*might*—have had somebody in my place. Maybe I wasn't as careful as usual. I did leave in a hurry this morning, to meet the girls at

Daisy's Diner."

"Do you honestly think that's what this is, Serena? Tell the truth."

She huffed out a sigh. "Fine. But I'll only go for a day or two. Since it's the weekend, I can move a couple of things around. But I've got to work on Monday. I'm not going to cancel my appointments because I'm being paranoid."

Antonio moved closer and picked up her hands in his. He didn't miss the slight trembling or how cold they felt. She was more scared than she'd admit, even though she tried to put on a brave front. If he didn't already know what she was hiding, he'd probably have missed the signs. Lifting one hand, he brushed a light kiss against her knuckles, watched her eyes widen at his surprise move.

"Let me make a couple calls and get everything set. By the time I'm done, I bet Rafe and his team will be finished, and you can pack enough for a couple days. Okay?"

She gave a sharp nod and pulled her hands free, wrapping her arms across her middle. With unhurried movements, he stood and walked back into the kitchen, pulling out his cell phone along the way. His first call was to his momma. Serena would be safe with her. She'd watch over her like a mama bear protecting her cub, and he couldn't think of better hands to handle Serena's care.

Serena watched Antonio walk away, her mind racing. Too much had happened today. She'd been thrown for a loop at the diner when Beth had mentioned Big Jim and the possibility he'd get a new trial. It didn't take a rocket scientist to figure out the feds would be hot on her trail again, wanting her to rehash in agonizing detail at the family dynamics and drama she'd run from in the first place. Then to come home and find her privacy had been violated. Somebody had found her, and her past was nipping at her heels.

Every survival instinct screamed for her to run. But it felt like she'd been running her whole life, and she was tired. Tired of hiding, changing her appearance, her name, her very identity because she'd done the right thing. Even now, she felt like she was the guilty party, because she'd been the one who'd ended up punished. Living in a prison of her own making, because she'd turned her back on her family, and trusted the government to keep their word, and keep her safe.

The way she lived wasn't living, merely existing, always looking over her shoulder, waiting for a sign she'd been found. Ready to run at any hint her uncle or one of his followers was onto her. Living in Shiloh Springs, she'd finally felt like she'd found a little peace. She'd even started to believe she might have a future, a life with the man she found fascinating, and a family who made her feel like she belonged.

She should have known it was too good to be true. Looking around her townhouse, it sank in she didn't have anything here she'd miss once she hit the road. Her worldly possessions would fit into one bag, and even then if she had to, she could leave it all behind and not miss anything. The clothing she wore was simply a façade, part of the persona she'd adopted to go along with the profession she'd found. Easily replaced with her next iteration—like a chameleon, she'd change and blend with her surroundings, adapt and survive.

Her go-bag was ready in the back of the master bedroom closet. Early on, she'd figured out keeping one handy saved her a lot of time and gave her fewer headaches when she needed to make a quick getaway. She'd fallen out of practice the last year, had gotten complacent. Soft—she'd grown soft and ill-prepared because she'd allowed herself to feel.

When Rafe walked into the living room, she stood and met him halfway. "Are you finished?"

He nodded. "We've taken prints and swept your bedroom and the other one. You didn't notice anything missing?"

"No. Just out of place. I'm starting to wonder if it's my imagination playing tricks." The look he shot her stopped her for spewing any more lies. It was clear he wasn't buying them anyway.

"I think you should stay someplace else until we figure out what exactly is going on."

Serena gave a harsh chuckle. "You and your brother think alike. He's in the kitchen calling the Big House and making arrangements for me to stay there over the week end."

Rafe smiled and crossed his arms over his chest, his eyes twinkling. "I was going to suggest the same. Momma will take good care of you, and you won't be alone. Plus, she'll stuff you full of good food. She'll love having somebody around to spoil, especially since Nica can't make it home like she planned."

The two techs paused in the doorway, and Rafe walked the few steps to meet them, and she watched them talk for a few seconds. She couldn't hear what they said, but she didn't miss the evidence bags in their hands, or the look of compassion Judith shot her way before she headed out the door.

Antonio roughly ran a hand through his hair. "Douglas will be here in a couple minutes."

"That's not necessary. I can drive myself—"

"He insisted." Antonio's mulish expression had her closing her mouth against further protest. It wouldn't do any good. He'd simply pick her up and haul her out to the truck like a sack of potatoes when his father got there if she argued. She'd like to keep what little dignity she had left.

"Rafe, we still need to talk. I'll give you a ride back to the station, if you don't mind waiting a few more minutes." Rafe gave a brief jerk of his head, and walked outside with the other tech.

Antonio walked over and stood close enough she could reach out her hand and touch him. And she wanted to. She wanted to feel his arms wrapped around her, pulling her close. She ached to feel his lips against hers, wild and unbridled, and finally unleash the passion she'd kept buried deep. If her days were numbered, she wanted to be wild and free, at least once in her life, and he was the man she'd secretly yearned for since the moment they'd met.

When his hand reached out and cupped her cheek, she closed her eyes, savoring the feel of his calloused skin against hers. She leaned into his touch, realizing she needed it, wanted it with her last breath. If this was all she could get, she'd take it and cherish the memory. The movement of his thumb against her cheek in a gentle caress made her gasp, the sound loud in the silent room.

"Serena, I..."

"Dad's here," Rafe's voice boomed from the doorway, shattering the moment, and Serena's eyelids sprang open, her eyes scanning Antonio's face. Whatever he'd been about to reveal was gone, his inscrutable mask firmly back in place.

"Listen to Dad, and do what he says. I'll be out later tonight." He paused, looking like he wanted to add more, then glanced away. "We have a few things we need to discuss."

"Alright."

"Serena, promise me you'll stay."

Her eyes flew to his face, trying to determine if there was some underlying meaning to his words. No, she was reading too much into things. He couldn't possibly know her secret.

"Please."

She nodded without thinking, because of one little word. Antonio never begged, never yielded, and yet he'd added a single please. How could she say no? Even if she ended up regretting it, she'd stay until she had no other choice.

CHAPTER TEN

"Williamson, we've got a situation."

"What kind of situation? You've barely started looking into the Berkley case. Have you found something already?"

Antonio scrubbed a hand over his face, and looked at his brother across his desk. After leaving Serena's townhouse, he'd driven Rafe back to the sheriff's office. He'd planned on explaining things to Rafe earlier, before they'd gotten the call about the break-in at Serena's, and there hadn't been time since. So, he'd done the next best thing. He'd followed Rafe into his office, closed the door, and put in a call to the special agent in charge of the case, putting the phone on speaker. Letting Rafe listen in would get him up to speed, and he needed to let Williamson know he was bringing the county sheriff in on the case as more than a consultant.

"First, I've got this call on speaker. I'm in the sheriff's office. We need to bring him in on this case." Rafe quirked his brow, but didn't say anything.

"Any particular reason you're bringing the sheriff in on an FBI assignment, Boudreau?"

"Several, which I'll explain, if I may?"

He heard Williamson sigh. "This is gonna be good. Go ahead, Boudreau. Make my weekend."

Antonio bit back a chuckle. Williamson sounded tired. He didn't blame him, the Austin FBI office was woefully understaffed, and their case load had exploded. And he was about to load even more bad news onto the other man's shoulders.

"First things first. SAC Derrick Williamson, meet Rafe Boudreau, sheriff of Shiloh Springs."

"Rafe Boudreau? Any relation?"

"My brother." Antonio watched Rafe across the table, noted the amused expression on his face.

"Good to meet you, Williamson. Hope Antonio isn't giving you too much grief."

"Other than disturbing the first Saturday I've had off in six weeks, he's okay. You have any idea what his big news is?"

"Not a clue."

"Alright then, Antonio, what's going on?"

"I should tell you, I may have a conflict of interest in this case. Once I explain, if you want to pull me off and reassign it to somebody else, I'll understand."

He watched his brother straighten in his chair, his attention fully focused and directed at him. Antonio could read the question in his gaze, and he gave a nonchalant shrug, waiting for Williamson's response.

"This day keeps getting better and better. Spit it out,

Boudreau."

"Turns out, I know Sharon Berkley."

"What?" The voices were like a choreographed duet, both Rafe and Williamson's question echoing through the speaker.

"Explain." Williamson's command came through loud and clear.

"I went through the info you provided on the Berkley case, both Big Jim and Sharon. I didn't look at her file until late this morning." He paused for a second before opening the file, sliding it across Rafe's desk, and pointed to the photo. "I recognized Sharon Berkley immediately."

"What? How?"

"Sir, the woman in the photo, Sharon Berkley, has been living in Shiloh Springs for almost a year under a different name. She looks different than in the photo, of course. She's changed her hair color, obviously wears colored contacts, but there's no denying it's her."

Rafe's head shot up, his expression perplexed. Antonio knew exactly how he felt, since he'd already run the gamut of emotions ever since he'd seen Sharon's face staring back at him from the FBI photograph.

"Serena?" he mouthed. Antonio nodded, still listening to Williamson's muttered curses.

"I guess that explains why you've brought your brother into the mix, since he knows her too. Have you taken her into custody?"

KATHY IVAN

"No. There's been an…incident."

"What kind of incident and do I really want to know?"

"Somebody may have broken into Serena's, um, Sharon's, townhouse today. We're checking it out, and the crime scene team has taken fingerprints. There's nothing definitive, but it's possible one of Big Jim's associates may have discovered she's living in Shiloh Springs."

"All the more reason to bring her in. We can relocate her, get her back into witness protection, and prepped for her testimony against James Berkley."

Antonio stood, because sitting was making him antsy. He walked several steps across the office, turned and paced back in the opposite direction. How was he going to convince Williamson it was in Serena's best interests to stay in Shiloh Springs? She'd been in witness protection twice, and even though Williamson had told him the feds leak had been plugged, who was to say another one wouldn't spring open if enough money changed hands? Putting Serena's safety into somebody else's safekeeping didn't sit well. She was his. His responsibility. His family's friend. His—just his. Period.

"Mr. Williamson, Antonio's told me the basics of the case, but from what I understand, Serena, I mean Sharon, went into witness protection during and after Big Jim's trial, and at least twice she was located with assassination attempts, correct?"

Williamson sighed. "True. There was an agent, part of

86

WITSEC, who accepted bribes to reveal her location. Said former agent is now serving time in a federal facility himself."

"Until we are sure Serena's cover has been blown, I think it's safer to keep her here in Shiloh Springs. Hear me out," Rafe interjected when Williamson started to interrupt. "Shiloh Springs is a smaller town than say Austin, and we usually know when a stranger shows up. Right now, we've got Sharon, Serena—that's way too confusing, why don't we call her Serena since it's the name she's been using for the last year. Anyway, Serena is at my parents' house. She can be protected there. Trust me, there are a lot of Boudreaus who either live at the ranch, or can be roped into helping out, keeping an eye on Serena."

"I don't know. It seems like she'd be better off in federal custody for her own protection."

"Williamson, we need Serena's cooperation. Her testimony is tantamount to keeping Big Jim behind bars for good. Here, she's among friends, people who've come to care about her a great deal. Don't you think being here, instead of holed up in some hotel room for the next who knows how many months, would make her more cooperative?" Antonio watched in awe as his brother laid it out for the Special Agent in Charge. Who knew his brother was so silver-tongued?

"Serena doesn't know anybody in Shiloh Springs knows her true identity. I'll have to break it to her, and I can guarantee her first instinct is going to be to run. But if she's surrounded by friends, people she considers as close as family, making her feel safe, I can talk her into staying."

Rafe nodded at his brother's words, giving him a hand gesture as if telling him to keep talking. He hoped Williamson bought it, because he knew Serena wouldn't stick around if she knew the FBI was sending agents to pick her up. And if she heard her uncle was getting another trial, they'd be lucky if she didn't leave the country altogether this time.

"Sir, she trusts me. She trusts Rafe. She works for my mother. Living at the Big House, we can make sure there's somebody with her twenty-four/seven. If you want feds there, we can make it look like they're working on the ranch, so she won't be suspicious. It's a win-win. Serena stays safe and the feds know exactly where she is when it's time for her to testify."

"You've both made valid points. Is this some kind of Boudreau thing—tag team the other guy until you get what you want?"

Rafe laughed. "No, but if it works, we might put it into our repertoire."

"Antonio, I want reports every day. If there's even a hint somebody's found her, I'm yanking her into federal custody. Got it?"

"Yes, sir."

Williamson huffed out a long breath. "I hope I'm not making the biggest mistake of my career. Copy me on the break-in report."

"You've got it. I'll have it in your e-mail by end of the day." Antonio gave his brother a fist bump, ecstatic he'd won this round. Though he knew he had a lot of explaining to do, not only to Rafe, but to his family. They'd need to know the salient facts in order to keep Serena safe and protected, without making her feel suffocated. A big chore, but better than the alternative.

"Every day, Boudreau. I want a phone call every day with updates, or I'm pulling her out of there."

"Understood. Thanks."

He hung up and looked at Rafe. "That went well, don't you think?"

"I think you've stepped in a huge smelly pile of problems is what I think. Serena? Sweet little Serena is related to that rotten scum?"

"Blows your mind. Yet it explains a lot. Why she's always been a little reserved, never revealed much about her background. She passed a background check, because our mother always does one on new hires, even contractors. Guess she used a pretty darn good hacker for her ID."

Rafe stood and grabbed his hat. "I've got a couple things to do before I head home. Unless you want me to go to the Big House with you to talk to Serena?"

"No, I've got it. I'll figure out how to tell her by the time I get there." *I hope.*

"We'll watch over her, keep her safe."

Antonio walked out with Rafe and headed for his car. Somehow, in the next hour, he needed to come up with a logical explanation to clue Serena in he knew about her past, knew her real identity, and he was her brand spanking shiny new bodyguard until the whole Big Jim situation was resolved.

It was going to be a long night.

CHAPTER ELEVEN

"Guys, I still think this is going overboard." Serena stood by the passenger door as Douglas lifted her suitcase out of the trunk. "I'm perfectly fine staying at my place."

At Douglas' direct stare, she immediately closed her mouth. The big man didn't need to stay a word to get his message across. She was staying with him and Ms. Patti until they figured out who'd invaded her townhouse and searched her stuff, and that was final. With a single phone call, Douglas had shown up at her townhouse, taken her bag, and loaded her in his truck without a single word. Before he'd helped her into the truck, he'd pulled her into his arms and wrapped her in a big bear hug. Somehow, with his simple act, she'd felt loved, safe and secure. Like she belonged. And now it was all going to disappear—just like she was going to vanish into the night.

Was it any wonder she'd grown to adore this family? From the very beginning, Ms. Patti had taken her under her wing and treated her like she was one of their own. Serena had soaked up the attention and affection like a half-starved pup, because it was unfamiliar and yet wonderful. She'd never had anything in her life which even compared with what the Boudreaus had, a loving family. A family who cared about the people around them, wanted only the best for each person in their close-knit group. It was so different from what she'd grown up understanding a family was, and what it meant. The second there'd been trouble, the entire Berkley clan turned their backs on her without a second thought. Big Jim held control over them all, with a tight fist and an iron hand. A shudder ran through her at the thought of her uncle. People thought they understood what monsters were. They had no real clue. Thankfully, he was behind bars, hopefully for the rest of his life, and couldn't hurt her any more.

"Serena, Ms. Patti's waiting for you inside. I'll take your bag up to the guest room."

"Thank you, Douglas, for everything."

Before she'd made it halfway to the front door, Ms. Patti stood framed in the open doorway. Her diminutive body stood silhouetted in the filtered sunlight as she stepped forward onto the porch, the large white columns and two stories spread wide, and she had the impression the house held its arms open, welcoming her like the prodigal daughter who'd been gone for far too long. It almost felt like she was coming—home.

"Don't just stand there, come on in. I've got sweet tea and banana nut muffins hot from the oven." She looked past Serena toward her husband, and a gentle smile curved her lips upward. "I've packed a little something for you. It should tide you over 'til supper."

"Thank you, sweetheart." He dropped a kiss on her cheek as he strode past with the suitcase, and Ms. Patti's eyes followed his every move, a look filled with so much love it almost brought Serena to tears. Oh, if only she could have somebody feel like that about her someday. But she wasn't meant to be one of the lucky ones, no matter how much she'd hoped things might be different with Antonio. She'd given in to the wishful dreams of having a life with him, and now those dreams had fractured into a million tiny pieces.

"Looks like you've got a bit of a dilemma." Ms. Patti linked her arm through hers and patted it gently. "Sit down, and you can tell me all about it. Then we'll figure out exactly what we're going to do to fix things." With the determination of a drill sergeant, Ms. Patti marched her into the kitchen and seated her at the long table before Serena could open her mouth to say a word.

She wrapped her hands around the glass of iced tea, unsure where to start. The last time she'd had a sit down with Ms. Patti, she'd allowed the older woman to convince her to stay in Shiloh Springs, though her every instinct screamed to hightail it out of town. She should have followed through on her first option, because now she'd been hustled from her own home, practically shanghaied and overwhelmed by the testosterone of the Boudreau men, and moved summarily to the Big House before she could utter much more than a token protest.

Not like I'm going to protest if it means I can spend a little while longer with Antonio before my world turns to cow patties.

"Would it help if I told you I don't care about your past or what you're running from?" Ms. Patti slid into the chair across from hers, and placed a platter stacked high with banana nut muffins in the center of the table. "Sugar, there ain't a single thing you can tell me that's worse than what's rolling around inside your head right now. Whatever it is, we'll handle it together."

Serena breathed out a deep breath. If only it was easy. Simply tell Ms. Patti and things would magically be fixed, and poof, all her problems would disappear. Unfortunately, real life didn't work that way, at least not in her world.

"I'm not sure where to start."

"The beginning's usually best, but start where you're comfortable, and we'll fill in the blanks later." Ms. Patti reached across and placed a muffin in front of Serena. "I've always found stuffing my face full of sugar and carbs makes most problems a little less scary. Besides, I made too many and you've gotta help me get rid of some of these."

Serena laughed and started picking at the wrapper around the muffin. It was a miracle she'd gotten through life without somebody like Ms. Patti there to help smooth away all the ugly stuff. The woman had become more a mother to her than her biological mother had ever been.

"I guess the first thing I should tell you is Serena Snowden isn't my real name." *There, I said it out loud. No going back now.*

"I know. I'm the one who did a background check on you when you came to work for my company, remember?" The smirk on Ms. Patti's face raised the little hairs on the back of Serena's neck. How could she possibly have known? She'd paid a fortune to a black-hat hacker to create her new identity, and it should have been foolproof.

"Sugar, I knew from the moment you walked through the door there was more to you than somebody looking for a job. You were looking for roots, a place to settle, whether you realized it or not. I recognize the signs. Trust me, after all the boys who've been through this house over the years, I've learned how to recognize a lost soul when I see one."

Serena gave a ragged chuckle. "I thought I had everything covered. Shows how clueless I truly am."

"Hush."

"I can't believe you've known all along I'm a fraud. I—I can't stay here. I can—"

"You can sit right back down in your chair, that's what you can do. Rafe and Antonio think you need to be here, so you're staying. Besides, I could use another female around this place. Sometimes it gets a little much with all these men traipsing through at all hours. Nica drops by when she can, but she's up to her eyeballs with school, so visits have been few and far between lately."

Serena stared at the woman seated across the table, and

read the sympathy and understanding in her gaze. There was something else there too, but she couldn't put her finger on it.

"Okay. This is just between us, right?"

"I have the feeling Antonio's gonna want to know your story, but I won't say anything. Not until or unless you tell me it's okay. Except, if you're running from the law, I'm going to have to tell Rafe. I won't let your put his career in jeopardy." Ms. Patti's eyes narrowed for a moment, before she leaned back in her chair again. "Nope, I can't see you ever doing something illegal, at least not by choice."

"I didn't do anything wrong, Ms. Patti. I promise. Well, maybe it depends on a person's definition of wrong. Nothing against the law, unless you consider running away from witness protection breaking the law."

"Witness protection? Like federal government-mandated, new identity-type protection?"

Serena nodded. "I need to back up a bit. I told you my real name isn't Serena Snowden. It's Sharon. Sharon Berkley." She waited to see if Ms. Patti would react to her revelation. When she didn't so much as twitch a muscle, Serena continued. "My family has had lots of run-ins with the law, both local and federal. The biggest criminal of the bunch is my uncle. You might have heard of him—Big Jim Berkley?"

At her revelation, Ms. Patti's eyes widened, though she didn't say a word, simply motioned for her to continue.

"My uncle is a horrible man. Even the government doesn't realize the reach he has, or the number of people who blindly follow him. My parents, my cousins, aunts, everybody listened to every malicious word spewing from his lips like it was the gospel of the second coming. Even I believed him in the beginning. Until he started spewing so much hatred for people he considered enemies of his idea of freedom and justice. Jews, Muslims, Asians, blacks, no one was excluded from his poisonous vendetta. He felt he was one of the 'true' Americans and anybody who didn't follow his beliefs was an enemy of the people, and needed to be taught the error of their ways."

Ms. Patti took a long swallow of her tea, and set the glass gently on the table. "I remember reading about the manhunt for him after they blew up the synagogue in Amarillo. Isn't he responsible for more than bombings?"

"Yes. For a long while, nobody was safe from Big Jim's reach. He's careful and smart. He never writes anything down and doesn't use computers, at least not personally. Others do the dirty work for him, while he keeps his hands clean. Don't doubt for an instant he isn't the mastermind behind everything. He's a monster."

"Oh, Serena. I'm sorry you've had to deal with this."

Serena glanced down to see while she'd been talking, she'd completely destroyed the muffin. It lay in tiny pieces atop the wrapper. Funny, she hadn't even realized she'd done it.

"I honestly can't say there was any one single thing that opened my eyes, made me see the truth about him and the rest of the family. They blindly followed everywhere he led them. As far as I know, they still do. At least the ones who aren't in prison. I haven't talked to them since…" Her words trailed off as she thought back to the trial. "Anyway, little things started bothering me. The way he treated people he supposedly loved. His sister, his children. Even my mom. When he wanted somebody watched, all he had to do was snap his fingers, and he'd have a dozen volunteers genuflecting and begging to do his bidding. I knew it was only a matter of time before somebody got killed, either in one of the buildings his followers bombed, or one of them taking things too far with their threats and intimidation."

"Did you leave?" Ms. Patti's question was voiced softly, and Serena glanced up, noting the sympathy and understanding in her gaze.

"I wanted to. Heck, I probably should have. Instead, I went to the feds. The FBI."

"Good."

Serena laughed, and the sound rang hollow to her own ears. "That's what I thought. I told them what my uncle and his group was doing, and what their plans were. Big Jim wasn't content with small time attention anymore. He wanted to make a statement. One big enough so nobody could ignore him anymore, and would shoot him right to the top. Who knows how many people would have been hurt or killed? So I turned him in to the feds, but they said they needed proof—and I didn't have any. Nothing but what I'd seen and heard."

Ms. Patti scrubbed a hand over her face. "Lemme guess. They wanted you to go back in and get them proof."

"Bingo. I was stupid. Naïve, stupid and gullible. They spent days convincing me to go back to Big Jim's compound—what I'd taken to calling it—and find them something to hold up in court. They didn't understand Big Jim. Not at all. The man has the brain of a genius and the cunning of a shark. I mentioned he never personally puts anything on a computer. Doesn't mean he didn't use others to deal with his online activity, but nothing tangible the feds can track back to him. A couple of my cousins are experts when it comes to computers. Big Jim paid for them to go to M.I.T. so they could handle all his finances and investigative work online. If he made notes or wrote anything down, once the cousins finished entering the data, the paper evidence was immediately burned. Nothing could be traced back to Big Jim. And my word alone wasn't enough to even indict him."

Ms. Patti stood and quickly cleaned up the mess Serena had made of the muffin, and swept it into the trash. Placing another muffin in front of Serena, she resumed her seat and placed another one in front of herself. "Knowing you, it didn't take much to convince you to go back in."

"I thought I could help. I hoped I'd be able to open the

eyes of some of my family, make them see my uncle for who he really is, not the beneficent patriarch he pretends to be. You have to understand, he's not your typical homegrown terrorist or religious zealot. He believes his own rhetoric, and is charismatic enough and rich enough for people to believe him."

"People like your uncle are more dangerous than most folks imagine, because they believe their own hype."

"Uncle James' family has money. Lots of money. The land's been in his family for generations, has gas and mineral rights, oil wells. Having wealth and power was never the real issue, although he loves to think he's more important any anybody else."

Serena curled her hands around her tea glass, because she'd already torn apart another muffin wrapper, and a pile of crumbs sat neatly stacked in a tidy mound. Ms. Patti must've noticed she needed something in her hands, to keep her talking, and handed her a kitchen towel. "You can tear this one up. I'm not too fond of it."

"I didn't have a problem being assimilated back into the fold. My parents are devoted to Uncle James. My dad worked with him closely, helping oversee the day-to-day management of the business. He's particularly good at balancing the books, though he's never been one of my uncle's favorites. I think there was some kind of falling out between them years ago, and he's never let my father forget about whatever happened. Always with subtle jabs, but I could tell there was history, if not outright animosity between them. My mother is Uncle James' stepsister."

"I did wonder at the family connection," Ms. Patti admitted. "Okay, they let you back into the bosom of the family. Then what?"

"I'm not proud of what I did, but I got close to one of my uncle's security guards."

"Close?"

Serena's head bowed and she nodded. "Nothing happened, but I led him on. Let him think I cared for him. I think he was going to propose, so I knew I had to get out of there fast." Her hands wrapped around the kitchen towel and she pulled it taut, nervous butterflies fluttering around in her belly. The last time she'd talked about any of this had been on the witness stand in one of the biggest trials in years.

"Sweetheart, if you want to stop—"

"No, Ms. Patti, you deserve the truth. You've been nothing but kind to me, and I've lied to you from the day we met. Let me get this out, so you know the truth. I've hated living a lie. You and Douglas, you've made me feel like a part of your family, a part of the community. I never had that before. My mother did whatever Uncle James asked, even if it meant leaving her child behind. She disappeared when I was little, running off and leaving me and my dad behind. My dad was a little better, but at least I saw him sometimes, when he wasn't bowing and scraping at my uncle's feet."

"I never knew how bad your childhood must have been."

"Don't feel sorry for me. There are lots of kids who have it worse." Serena smiled at Ms. Patti. "As you'd know firsthand, with all the boys who've made their way through the Big House over the years."

"Not the same thing, but, let's get back on track. You seduced the guard—"

"No! I didn't *seduce* him. It was…I used him to get information. That doesn't sound any better. I wasn't honest, I let him think I felt something for him when I didn't." She rubbed at the bridge of her nose, wishing she'd never started this conversation, but knowing she couldn't and wouldn't hide the truth from Ms. Patti. If she was being honest, Ms. Patti was her best friend, and she'd hated lying to her. At least now, everything would be out in the open. It felt like a weight had been lifted off her chest, one she hadn't even realized was there, and she felt freer.

"Pete was close to my uncle, which made it easier for me to be around when they talked. Uncle James never realized I was looking for evidence to bring his world crashing down around his ears. I think he got comfortable with my always being around, and sometimes forgot I was there. It's not hard to become invisible when you're in a room with a lot of people with big egos and even bigger mouths. Narcissists want and need to be the center of attention, and Uncle James is one of the biggest ones I've ever seen. It was like he fed off the attention."

"Which I'm guessing made him complacent."

"And careless." Serena took a long drink of her sweet tea, and closed her eyes as the coolness of the drink coated her parched tongue. She'd been talking enough her throat was dry, but she couldn't stop. Too close to all the truth being out there—finally.

"He never claimed responsibility for the bombings—any of them. As I said, he's meticulously careful about keeping his hands clean. With his money, he's never had trouble getting others to do his dirty work."

"But he obviously made a mistake, or you wouldn't be sitting here." Ms. Patti reached across and gave her hand a squeeze. "And I'm glad you're here, regardless of the circumstances. My family will take care of you."

Warmth spread through Serena at Ms. Patti's words. It started deep inside, and seemed to bubble up with her, a sensation she'd never felt before, strange and yet wonderful, because she realized what the feeling meant. She was loved.

"Thank you. You don't know how much you mean to me. I know I've never said, but you are the mother I never had growing up. When I showed up in Shiloh Springs, looking to start my life over, you welcomed me. Gave me a job. A second chance to make something of my life. You trusted me without knowing the first thing about me. There's no way I can ever repay your kindness."

"Love doesn't need to be repaid, honey. It's to be shared, without strings, without expectations. That's the thing about the heart. There is an amazing amount of love inside to be given, and the more you give, the more you get back in return."

Ms. Patti looked past her as she spoke, her gaze focused on something or somebody. She spun around, and Antonio stood in the open doorway.

"How long have you been standing there, son?"

"Long enough, Momma." He walked into the kitchen and put his hand on Serena's shoulder, his firm yet gentle touch sending a tingle down her spine. "I need to talk to Serena."

"Serena?" Ms. Patti's unasked question was reflected in her gaze.

"It's okay. Antonio's right, we need to talk." Serena rose and walked around the table, leaning in to hug Ms. Patti close, infusing all her love into the gesture. "Thank you again—for everything."

"Momma, is it okay if I take Serena to the garden?"

Ms. Patti froze for a second before her lips turned up in a smirk. "Absolutely. Give me a holler if you need anything."

Antonio held his hand out to Serena without a word. She slid hers into his grasp, and he led her from the kitchen. She swallowed nervously, feeling like a prisoner being led to the gallows. Great, she thought, now I'm doing gallows humor. Might as well quote *we who are about to die salute you*.

Antonio chuckled. "I promise, nobody's going to die."

She blushed, realizing she'd spoke her thoughts aloud. "Good. I'm too tired to defend myself."

"We're only going to talk. I think it's past time for both of us to be honest, don't you?"

CHAPTER TWELVE

Antonio led Serena around the side of the house and across the patio. She looked around at the chairs and table, along with pots holding a plethora of greenery thanks to his mother's green thumb. The spot was cozy, a place where he knew she'd spent many afternoons with his momma, sipping sweet tea and talking about work and whatever else women talked about when they got together and there weren't any men around.

Curiosity filled her expression when he kept going, past the patio and headed to a spot he knew she'd never been. A place reserved for family, one very few outside their close-knit clan were privileged with an invitation.

He guided her through a strand of tall pine trees several more yards before he stopped, giving her time to take in the idyllic scene, one that always filled him with a sense of awe. A conical-shaped, white-roofed gazebo sat in the center of a clearing. White lattice surrounded the bottom, with a circular roof perched atop the structure. Its graceful lines and angles of the structure blended into the surroundings like something from a fairy tale, the otherworldly beauty seeming unnatural yet inviting, the perfect escape deep in the heart of this spread of Texas earth. This was his mother's favorite spot on the ranch.

Intertwined around the base and pillars of the gazebo were climbing pink and white roses and ivy. Tall ornamental grasses lent to its fairy tale-like appearance. Inside the gazebo, at its heart, sat something even more surprising—a wishing well. Smooth stone and wood, its incongruous appearance should have been out of place on a working Texas ranch, yet somehow in Antonio's mind it fit.

Taking Serena's hand, Antonio led her to a white painted bench partially hidden away within the gazebo's walls. Tiny white lights wrapped around the tree bases, and along the inside of the roof. He flicked a switch by the entrance, and smiled as the lights turned on, the soft golden glow wrapping the entire place in beauty.

"What is this?" He heard the wonder in her voice, watched as she traced the petals of the roses. "I've never seen anything like it."

"Momma's secret garden. She loves this place."

"I never knew this was here. She must have spent years getting it to look like this."

Antonio nodded, joining Serena on the bench. "You ready to talk?"

When she looked at him with those big eyes, he swallowed hard. He tried to picture her without the colored contact lenses. Didn't matter, no matter what color her eyes were in his imagination, she still looked like his Serena. Her darker hair was windswept from the cool afternoon breeze, darker than her picture in his FBI file. Her eyes gleamed in the dappled sunlight shining through the gazebo's walls.

"I know everything, Serena."

He didn't think her eyes could get any bigger, but she proved him wrong, reminding him of the anime characters from comics he'd devoured as a teen. Her indrawn breath gave away her nervousness. "How?"

"Did you forget I work for the FBI?"

"Of course not."

He held on when she tried to pull her hand away, needing to keep contact between them, more for his own sanity than any real desire to keep her captive. Telling her what he knew was going to be hard enough, he didn't want a chasm between them.

"The case they assigned me when I came to the Austin office was to look for Sharon Berkley. Imagine my shock when I saw the photo in the case file. Different hair, contact lenses. At first, I didn't want to believe it. I didn't say anything to the special agent in charge of your case; instead, I hightailed it back to Shiloh Springs. I wanted to see with my own two eyes what my brain told me was fact."

"Why didn't you confront me right away? If you knew who I was—"

"This morning I got to Shiloh Springs, and went to see Rafe. I wanted to talk with him, figure out what I should do because I didn't trust my instincts. Before I could say anything, do anything, your townhouse was broken into. Should I have pounced on you the minute I crossed the threshold, told you the FBI wanted you back in protective custody? Even I'm not that much of a monster, Serena."

"So much has happened in such a short time, I guess I forgot we hadn't spoken in a while. But you could've taken me in, or had the FBI pick me up and put me back into protective custody. Why didn't you?"

Antonio looked down at their joined hands, needing to find the right words to convince Serena he was on her side. "I persuaded Williamson, he's the SAC on your case in Austin, you'd be safer staying at the Big House where we could keep you close, but still out of the public eye. We didn't have any idea Big Jim already knew you were in Shiloh Springs. Rafe and I talked to Williamson, because I'm still not totally convinced there isn't a leak further up the chain with the feds. How else could your uncle have found you?"

Serena pushed her hair behind her ear in an unconscious movement, her head dipped low. She was the most beautiful woman he'd ever seen. He wished for the millionth time they'd met under different circumstances. One where she wasn't on the run for her life. Where he wasn't the FBI agent whose job it was to bring her in, even if it meant keeping her safe. But those were the facts, and until he could figure a way around it, he needed to keep his emotions under check, no matter how much he wanted to pull her into his arms and shield her from everything the world tossed her way.

"I might have the answer to that." Her voice was barely above a whisper. "The magazine article about Boudreau Realty."

Antonio stared at her, trying to understand what she was talking about. He didn't know anything about a magazine article. "What article?"

"Didn't your mother tell you about it? Some interior design magazine did this thing about the top realty companies across the United States, and Ms. Patti's was one of the featured offices. I did my best to not be in when the photographer was there, but somehow I ended up in one of the pictures, which naturally was the one used. It's only a profile shot, but I'm there. It's the only thing I can think, because I've been super careful to stay out of the public eye for almost a year."

"You're probably right. I'll have Williamson check out the magazine. I can't picture Big Jim Berkley reading interior design magazines, though."

"Yeah, I don't think he's the type to read them, but maybe one of the women who follow him does."

"Good point."

Serena squeezed his hand tight, and he felt the slight tremble in hers. "Antonio, I'm scared."

"You know I'll never let anybody or anything hurt you ever again, right?"

She gave a shaky laugh. "I hate to burst your bubble, Captain Caveman, but you can't be with me all the time."

"Watch me."

"Be realistic. The best thing for everyone is to turn myself over to the FBI. Go into seclusion until I have to testify. Again." Pulling her hand free, she stood and walked over to stand at the entrance of the gazebo. Silhouetted against the backdrop of all Mother Nature's bounty, the tall pines, the delicate roses and climbing ivy, she appeared like an earth goddess, fragile yet with an inner strength which refused to be quenched by life's turbulent chaos.

"Serena, stay here. You'll be surrounded by people you know. People who care about you. Whenever I'm not here, somebody will be. There are enough Boudreaus around at any given time, you'll never be alone. Plus, I bet Momma would love to have another woman around the place. She's always complaining there's too much testosterone smothering her. I guarantee she'll spoil you."

"I want to, but I can't put your family in danger." He could almost hear the unspoken "*or you.*"

He stood and walked to stand beside her, needing to be closer. Everything in him screamed to hold her in his arms, protect her from anybody or anything trying to harm her, but he resisted the impulse. He knew she was off balance by the day's events and here he was, springing the news that her cover had been blown. He spoke softly, keeping his tone gentle. "Before you argue any further, let me tell you what

I've done. I've set it up some safeguards so there's always somebody here when I'm not around. All my brothers, Dad, off-duty officers from the sheriff's department. If I need to, I'll have the FBI send a couple of people to assist, but rest assured you are not going to be alone. Big Jim's people aren't getting anywhere near you."

"Antonio, you can't—"

"Serena, even if this wasn't my job, I would move heaven and earth to keep you safe. Haven't you figured that out yet?"

Her eyes searched his face, surprise and hope in her gaze. "I don't know what to say."

"Don't say anything, except you'll be careful, and you won't leave the Big House without me or somebody with you. Promise me."

After a short pause, she nodded. "Okay. Thank you."

He clasped both of her hands between his, and ran his thumb across her knuckles, the gesture soft and gentle, before he led her back to the bench. "Can I tell you something? It might help explain why I'm being a smidge overprotective."

"Of course."

"You know I'm adopted. Douglas and Ms. Patti are the best parents anybody could ask for. Loving, kind, they gave out hugs when they were needed, and discipline when I screwed up."

"Everybody talks about the Boudreaus in Shiloh Springs.

I can't remember anybody ever saying a bad word about Douglas or Ms. Patti. When I first moved here, I almost thought they walked on water, the way people described them. Too good to be true. There had to be a catch somewhere. Only there isn't one. With them, everything I heard is true. What they portray to the community is exactly who they are out of the public eye when nobody is watching. I love that about them."

"They epitomize the best of humanity. When I came to stay with them, Rafe and Brody already lived here. Things were…" he paused, choosing his words carefully, "rocky in the beginning. Being from New York, I wasn't the easiest kid to get along with. Add in the hormones of puberty, a chip on my shoulder the size of a boulder, and a 'don't mess with me' attitude, I wasn't the perfect candidate when Dad and Momma took me in."

Serena scooted a little on the bench, until her thigh pressed against his, and leaned her head against his shoulder. "It's hard to imagine you as a kid. I bet you were a handful. How'd you end up in Texas?"

"That's a long story, and I'll tell you everything another time, but the short version is my mother fell in love with somebody her family didn't approve of, sort of a Romeo and Juliet affair. Only instead of the Montagues and the Capulets, we're talking the two biggest crime families in New York and New Jersey."

Her hands twisted in his grip until she now held his, and

she squeezed them reassuringly, silently urging him to go on.

"You can imagine how that went over between the two groups. My mom was told in no uncertain terms she couldn't see my father anymore. My dad's family gave him the same ultimatum. The infighting got worse, until my mom dropped the bombshell she was pregnant."

"Oh, boy."

"Yeah, it wasn't a match made in heaven. My parents didn't care, they were stupid kids in love, and thought the whole world revolved around them. They were too young and too naïve to realize things didn't always work out the way you plan. My mother's father was a *consigliere,* or counselor, for the family, part of the upper tier without actually being part of the violence. My mother getting pregnant by a rival family member brought shame to the family."

"Nonsense."

"No, Italian mob. We're talking years ago, when things were a lot different, when the balance of power was delicate and earned with violence and bloodshed." He lifted their entwined hands and placed a gentle kiss on the back of hers. "My father wasn't high in the hierarchy. Basically, he was a snot-nosed kid, and his family had ties to the organization. His maternal cousin ties to the don. But he was a good man involved in a lot of bad stuff. Growing up, I was sheltered from a lot of it, but you aren't raised in that culture without grasping the subtle and not-so-subtle nuances of violence and people disappearing all the time."

"It must have been awful."

"Sometimes. Most of the time I played with my cousins like any other kid, even though I wasn't allowed to go outside as much as the other kids. My parents weren't allowed to marry, the families forbade it. My father visited when he could, and my mom loved me and made sure I knew how much my dad loved me too." He tried to remember his mother's face, her sweet smile and perfumed hugs. A lot of time had passed, years spent with the Boudreaus filled with love and compassion and a whole different kind of family.

"When I turned nine, tensions escalated between the two families, disputes over power and territory. My mom knew I'd be sucked into that world if she didn't do something. She had money, cash she'd socked away for years. Maybe she had a premonition of what might happen, but we took off one night. Didn't tell anybody, simply walked out with the clothes on our backs, and fled."

"Antonio, it must have been so scary. No child should have to deal with living like that."

"I know. She did it to protect me. She didn't want me dragged into a world of violence and crime, and knew if we stayed there wouldn't be any other option for me. I was already being taught to hate my father's family. This grudge, battle, whatever you want to call their struggle for dominance in the Italian districts, bled over into every aspect of life. It informed every decision, every action, and she loved me so much." He stopped, drawing in a deep breath. He needed to cut to the chase, and tell her the hard part before he chickened out. Living with the Boudreaus, he didn't have to talk about or rehash his early years; they'd accepted him the way he was, without prejudice or censure. Most families wouldn't want to responsibility or possible danger of bringing a child of the mafia into their home, but Douglas and Ms. Patti hadn't even blinked, instead sheltering him and giving him the kind of stability he'd craved.

"We left New York with nothing. Took the subway to Connecticut. My mom bought a used car and we headed anywhere outside New York. New Jersey was out of the picture, too. I didn't find out until weeks later the reason we left in the dead of night was because my mom got a message smuggled in from a friend. My father had been killed, and the inevitable battle between the families loomed. Getting me away was the only thing she knew to do to keep me alive."

"I'm glad she did," Serena whispered, her head still snuggled onto his shoulder. "I guess we have more in common than I thought. We both come from unconventional families, who don't have any problem bending the law to suit their own purposes."

"True."

"Tell me the rest. How'd you end up with Douglas and Ms. Patti?"

"Mom did her best to stay off the radar. Paid cash. We drove from state to state. I don't think she planned on staying in Texas long. We'd stopped for the night at some crappy motel. There was a convenience store across the street, and she left me in the room while she went to grab us some stuff for dinner, and snacks for the next day. I—I wanted to go with her, but she told me she'd just be a minute. If I'd gone with her, maybe I could have saved her, done something. She was killed in a botched robbery. Some druggie needed cash for a fix, and held up the store while she was there." He closed his eyes against the painful memory, the one filled with sirens and screams.

"I'm so, so sorry, Antonio."

"It was a nightmare. Cops, social workers, paramedics. Chaos. Everything blended together, sights and sounds, and I couldn't focus on anything. They'd sat me in the back seat of a police car with the door open. Then this giant of a man walked up to me, looked me right in the eye, like he was searching from something. He didn't say a word, but watched me for the longest time. Finally, he held out his hand, and I took it."

"Douglas?"

Antonio smiled. "Yep. One of the paramedics worked with him before, when they got Rafe. Said there was something about me, some instinct or whatever, which made him call Douglas. He and Ms. Patti pushed through all the paperwork and red tape to get me into their home. You know the rest."

"I'm sorry you lost your parents, Antonio, though I'm happy you ended up with Douglas and Ms. Patti. Without them, I don't think you'd be the man you are. A man with compassion, integrity, and honor."

"I've been blessed. There's a whole lot more to the story with my biological family, but it can wait for another time. We need to get you settled in."

"Wait, I do have one question. Your last name is Boudreau. Douglas and Ms. Patti adopted you?"

Antonio relaxed and wrapped his arm around her shoulders. "No, between the state and information obtained from sources, it was decided it would be too dangerous to adopt me. Adoption meant bringing my whereabouts to the attention of the very people my mother was running from."

"Then how—"

"It's kind of a tradition amongst us. Rafe started it, and the rest of us did it, too. When we turned eighteen, and could legally do it, we changed our last name to Boudreau. Partly out of respect and admiration for the people who raised us, and partly because we are a family. I'm honored to carry the name Boudreau. I wasn't born with it, but it's mine by choice, and I'm proud to be part of this amazing family."

They stood, and Antonio brushed the hair back from her cheeks, tempted beyond words to pull her into his arms and kiss her until they were both breathless, but knew the time wasn't right. She'd been hit with a lot, an overload of information, along with the threat of her uncle. He'd give her time to adjust, to think about what he'd told her. But not too much time, because he intended Serena to be in his life for the long haul, forever.

She just didn't know it yet.

CHAPTER THIRTEEN

"**N**o, I'm happy to help, Mr. Olson. I can meet you there in thirty minutes, if that works for you?"

"Wonderful, Serena. I've had my eye on this piece of property for the past three years, and heard they listed it this morning. Didn't even call me, like they promised, which ticks me off, but what am I gonna do, right? I'm afraid if I wait, somebody is going to snatch it up before I can even see it or make an offer."

"It's no problem. I'll pull the details and contact the agent representing the property, and see what we can do about making a deal, okay?"

"I know I can always count on you, Serena. See you there."

Serena stared at her phone, feeling a bit guilty. She'd promised Antonio she wouldn't leave the Big House without one of the Boudreaus or somebody from the sheriff's department going with her. Ridge was around somewhere, having been dragged into being her babysitter today. She knew she should let him know where she was going, but he'd insist on tagging along, and she didn't want to upset a client by bringing somebody along on their walk-through. Mr. Olson was a good client, and she'd been dealing with him exclusively since she'd moved to Shiloh Springs. He'd been her very first sale with Boudreau Realty, and they'd done a few transactions since then, mostly with rental properties he owned and the company managed. Between the trip to visit this prospective property and getting back, she wouldn't be gone more than a couple hours tops. Besides the commission would add a nice chunk to her bank account, and she'd need the money if she had to take off and start over again.

For a second, she contemplated shooting Antonio a text, but he'd try to convince her to stay put. Honestly, she was going a bit stir crazy. Everybody had been over-the-top nice, but being around so many people kept her already frazzled nerves on edge. She was used to living alone, and missed having some quiet time all to herself. Grabbing a pen, she scribbled a quick note, and stuck it to the fridge with one of the cute magnets Ms. Patti collected. With a quick move, she grabbed her purse, shoved the phone inside, and sprinted for the door. So far, so good. No sign of Ridge.

Once on the road, she glanced in the rearview mirror, the Big House fading away in the background. A twinge of remorse assailed her, but she shook it off. Darn it, she wasn't a prisoner, and she wouldn't feel guilty for leaving without telling anybody. She was a grown adult, and could come and go as she pleased. Besides, she needed to do her job if she wanted to be able to make her mortgage payment and pay her bills.

Tapping the button on the steering wheel, she turned on the radio. A country music oldie poured forth and she smiled. She'd never admit it in a million years, but since moving to Shiloh Springs, she'd grown to love country music, especially the older stuff. Humming along with the melody, she studied the road ahead. Since it was the middle of the afternoon, there wasn't a whole lot of traffic to contend with, and she should be right on time for her meeting with Mr. Olson.

She drove a couple of miles, her fingers tapping on the steering wheel to the rhythm of the next song. Staring through the windshield, she noted a car headed toward her. They had to be going to the Big House, because theirs was the only property on this stretch of road from Shiloh Springs. As it drew closer, she noted it was a dark sedan, one she didn't readily recognize. The Big House had lots of folks coming and going all the time, so it wasn't unusual she didn't recognize the car. The Boudreaus were well liked in their community, and people stopped by all the time to talk with Ms. Patti and Douglas.

The sedan continued getting closer and was almost even with her when it swerved into her lane. Her foot slammed on the brake and her car fishtailed on the pavement, swerving sharply to the right. It skittered off the asphalt and onto the rocks and grass bordering the road. Hands gripped tight around the steering wheel, she struggled to straighten the car, and felt a rocking jolt as the other car sideswiped hers. Her body jolted against the seatbelt, and the back end of her car slid down into the culvert beside the road. It lurched to a sudden stop, and the airbags deployed, with an explosion of powder. Her body slammed forward into the airbag, the seatbelt strap taut against her chest.

It took a few seconds for it to sink in, to realize what happened. She blinked furiously, trying to dispel the powder from the exploding airbag, and swatted ineffectively at the deflating fabric. The ringing in her ears obliterated all sound, and she coughed, reaching for her seatbelt. Every move hurt, her body screaming in protest to each movement.

She glanced frantically around the front seat, searching for her purse. Her instincts screamed to find her phone and call for help. The purse lay on the floorboard on the passenger side, its contents spilled and tossed in every direction. Leaning over the center console, muscles scream-ing in protest, she reached forward, her fingers scrambling for the cell phone. She needed to call for help—she needed Antonio. Too bad the darned thing was out of reach. The tips of her fingers barely brushed against the cool metal case, only succeeding in moving it a little further away.

Straightening in her seat, she took a deep breath, and latched onto the door handle. The other driver, she needed to check and see if they'd been injured. She hadn't noticed anybody else in the car, but because she hadn't seen anybody didn't mean there wasn't. Everything happened too fast for her to be sure. Pulling on the handle, she pushed, but the door refused to budge. Bracing herself for the pain she knew was coming, she rammed her shoulder against the door, trying to force it open. No use.

Something sticky and wet trickled into her eye, and she touched it. Her hand came away with bright red blood coating her fingertips. Using the back of her arm, she whisked away the dripping blood with her sleeve. Looking around, she tried to figure out how to get out of the car. The windshield was intact, so she couldn't climb out, and she definitely wasn't strong enough to break it from the inside. Which meant she had to climb out the passenger side.

Great.

Maneuvering across the center console and onto the passenger seat took a lot longer than she'd thought it would, muscles screaming with every movement, but finally she managed to grab onto the door handle and push the door open. Sliding across the seat, she swung both legs out the open door, only stopping long enough to grab her cell phone.

On shaky legs, she stood, and a wave of dizziness swamped her, and she latched onto the doorframe hoping it would pass. She rubbed absently at the center of her chest, right along where the seatbelt strap hit her torso. It had probably saved from a whole lot worse injuries, but it was beginning to ache.

Bracing herself on the car, she shuffled her way around

the back end of the car, slipping and sliding a couple of times on the muddy roadway shoulder. The black sedan who'd hit her blocked both sides of the road, the engine dead. The front of the car faced away from her, and she couldn't see the driver. Gingerly, she made her way to the passenger side, and peered inside.

A dark-haired man sat slumped over in the driver's seat, facing away from her. His body rested against the steering wheel. It didn't appear the airbag had deployed. One arm rested atop the steering wheel, while the other dangled at his side. Knocking on the passenger window to get his attention, she watched, but he didn't move. Maybe he was unconscious?

Serena made her way around to the driver's side. The entire front driver's side was crushed, the wheel well caved in, the tire flattened from the impact. Jagged gouges from the crash scraped along the driver's door, and she prayed she'd be able to get it open and help the injured man.

"Sir, are you okay?"

The driver slowly raised his head and she got the first clear look at his face and gasped. Mixed feelings of recognition and dread coiled deep inside. Her first instinct was to run away, as fast as her legs could carry her, because once he saw her face, any hope of remaining in Shiloh Springs unrecognized disappeared like a puff of smoke. Despite her trepidation, she couldn't leave him. What if he was hurt—or worse? She'd never forgive herself if she ran away and left him to die.

"Jonathan?" As gently as she could, she reached through the shattered window, and eased him back against the seat. He groaned, the sound pain-filled, though she couldn't see any blood. When he turned to look at her, she saw the moment recognition struck. He tried to move, and moaned in pain.

"Sharon, is it really you? Or am I hallucinating?"

"Sit still, I'm going to call nine-one-one. Help will be here soon."

"I wouldn't do that, Sharon."

She looked up at his words, her fingers hovering over the keypad. The gun in his hand pointed straight at her. She didn't know a lot about guns, but she'd watched enough television and movies to recognize a nine-millimeter, knew the damage it could do at close range.

"Jonathan, what are you doing? Let me call for help—"

"Toss the phone on the ground. Now. Don't make me hurt you." He shoved his shoulder against the car door, and it opened. Keeping the gun trained on her, he unhooked the seatbelt and climbed from the driver's seat. Instinctively, she took a step back, before stopping in her tracks at his angry scowl.

"I'm won't ask again, Sharon. Toss the phone on the ground."

Knowing she didn't have a choice with the gun pointed at her, she complied. Her gut tensed when he rammed his heel against the phone, crushing it. He gave it a second stomp, making sure the screen cracked beneath his shoe.

I can't stand here and let him shoot me. I'm not ready to die. Not without ever getting the chance to tell Antonio how I feel.

"What are you going to do? Shoot me in the middle of the street? There's not a lot of traffic on this road, but it won't be long before somebody comes by and sees us."

"I didn't mean to hit you quite so hard. You're okay. My car isn't going anywhere. We'll have to take yours." He looked at her Camry, partway off the road on the shoulder, then glanced at his. "It's a rental, so no big loss. Not in my name, anyway." He took a step toward her. "You're a very hard person to find, Sharon. Or is it Serena now?"

"I'll never be Sharon Berkley again."

"You're right, you won't. Big Jim is very unhappy with you. He wants you dead."

"And he sent you?"

Jonathan shook his head, chuckling at some private joke. "Hardly. Last time I saw your uncle, I told him where you were. He ordered me to put a hit on you."

Serena swallowed at his words. If her uncle knew where she was, she was as good as dead. He'd never tolerated anybody going against the family, or more importantly, him. To do so had been the ultimate act of betrayal, and he'd never let it stand.

"You decided to do the job yourself?"

"Nope. Your uncle has gone 'round the bend in a big way. He's crazy as a loon, and I want out from under his thumb. You're my ticket to freedom, Sharon, and I intend to cash in, and I'll never have to deal with Big Jim or anybody like him ever again."

"I don't understand."

"Of course you don't. Get in the car and I'll explain everything, but we need to get out of this Podunk town before the locals show up. You drive, since you know the roads, and the quickest way back to civilization."

Serena's brain raced, trying to come up with a plan. If she got in the car with Drury, there was a one hundred percent chance she'd end up a corpse. There had to be another option. She took a step toward her Camry. The driver's door wouldn't open. She'd had to climb over the center console to get out, which meant Drury couldn't get the driver's door open, either.

"You're going to have to drive. My vision's still blurry from banging my head, I'm afraid I'll crash."

She heard Drury murmur something under his breath, before spinning her around. "Don't try anything stupid, Sharon. I've got nothing to lose at this point, because if your uncle finds out what I'm doing, he'll kill me right after he slits your throat."

He shoved her and she stumbled forward, catching herself before face-planting on the asphalt. Drury was steps behind her as they headed around to the passenger side. She only had one shot at this, and her timing had to be perfect. As Drury braced his hand against the door frame and began looking inside the car, she pushed the passenger door closed with all her might, slamming it on his hand. Too bad it wasn't the hand holding the gun, but she had to hope the pain was enough to distract him.

Drury let out a shout of pain as the door collided with his wrist, cursing a blue streak. Serena didn't wait around to see what he'd do. Instead, she took off running toward the trees along the side of the roadway. She sprinted between them, her legs pumping, her breath soughing in and out of her chest as she ran. Her only thought—get as far away from Drury as she could and find someplace to hide.

Behind her, she heard footsteps crunching on the ground, the dead leaves littering the dirt magnifying each step. But she didn't dare stop running, because that meant certain disaster. Drury thought her uncle was insane, but she wasn't convinced they shouldn't be sharing side-by-side padded cells in the loony bin. She had no idea where she was headed, but it didn't matter. The only thought she could focus on was keeping each foot in front of the other, and putting distance between her and the man with the gun.

More curses filled the air, and they sounded a lot closer. Serena didn't dare look back. He was gaining on her, and even with the adrenaline coursing through her veins, her body was tiring. The trauma from the accident, combined with the sudden burst of activity, rapidly drained what little energy she had left. She struggled to keep running, moving forward.

Must get far away from the man with the gun. I don't want to die.

Drawing in as much air as she could, she put on a burst of speed, sprinting toward a large patch of overgrown bushes. If she could get behind them, she'd have a chance at hiding. She stumbled forward as her foot caught on something, and landed hard, knocking the air out of her. Yet she struggled to keep going, crawling and dragging her worn-out body the last few feet, until the deep green foliage screened her from Drury's view. Her palms were crusted with dirt, and she used the back of one hand to swipe at her forehead, which had started bleeding again after her fall.

Frantic, she looked around her, searching from something—anything—she could use as a weapon. It wouldn't do much good against a nine-millimeter, but she wasn't giving up without a fight. She wanted to live. She wanted an end to the running and hiding. She wanted a life with Antonio because she loved him. And if she got the chance, she'd make sure he knew how she felt.

Wrapping her hand around a thick branch, she curled up behind the bushes, making herself as small a target as possible. And prayed Antonio would find her—before it was too late.

CHAPTER FOURTEEN

Antonio's cell phone vibrated on his belt, where he'd clipped it earlier. He'd turned off the ringer while he met with Rafe. The fewer interruptions the better, because he needed to concentrate on Serena, and figure out a way to extricate her from the mess she was in. SAC Williamson was on his way to Shiloh Springs, at Antonio's insistence. He wanted to explain Serena's situation face-to-face, and have the man meet her in person. Let him realize she was more than an FBI file, a case to be closed and shuffled off to those higher up the food chain.

"Hey, Ridge, what's up?"

"Bro, we've got a problem. I came in from the barn, and found a note for you on the fridge from Serena. She's gone."

"Gone? What do you mean, she's gone?"

"She left to meet a client. Says she'll be back in a couple hours. I swear, I wasn't in the barn more than fifteen, twenty minutes tops. She must have snuck off while I was there."

Antonio rubbed the bridge of his nose between his thumb and finger. The headache he'd fought all morning roared into full force, fueled by anger, adrenaline, and fear.

Attorneys for the Justice Department had held a press conference earlier, covered by the national news, stating Big Jim Berkley had been granted a new trial, and the press was having a field day, rehashing all the facts from the previous trial. Serena's identity wouldn't be a secret much longer, once the good folks of Shiloh Springs saw the pictures on the internet and on TV of Sharon Berkley. He needed to get to her ASAP.

"Does the note say which client she's meeting?"

"No. I'm heading out now, see if I can catch up to her." Worry laced Ridge's voice. "She knew she wasn't supposed to go anywhere without one of us. Why didn't she wait? Or come get me. I wasn't far away."

"Do me a favor first. Call Mom's office, see if they know who she's meeting. I'll head toward the Big House, see if I can catch her before she gets too far."

"Will do. I'll let you know what I find out."

Antonio hung up and walked into Rafe's office. "We've got a problem. Serena's on her way into town."

Rafe raised a brow. "Ridge with her?"

"Nope. She left a note, saying she needed to meet a client. He found it and called me. I'm going to head back toward home, see if I can catch up to her. Ridge is calling Mom's office to see if we can determine who she's supposed to meet. Then he's going to head this way. Between us, maybe we'll catch up to her before—"

"Hang on, I'll go with you." Rafe grabbed his hat,

shoved his cell phone in his pocket, and headed for the door. After a quick conversation with Sally Anne, who was covering the front desk, they piled into Rafe's car and headed toward the Boudreau ranch.

They rode is silence for several minutes, and the knot in Antonio's gut grew with each passing mile. He thought he'd convinced Serena to sit tight, let them look out for her, until he and Williamson could figure out how to keep her safe. He hadn't spoken with Williamson since the news of Big Jim's new trial broke. Now more than ever it was imperative to keep Serena safe, because her testimony was the only thing keeping Big Jim behind bars, where he belonged.

"Bro, slow down. It won't help Serena if we end up splattered on the asphalt."

Antonio ignored his brother's comments, his foot pressing harder against the accelerator. He had a bad feeling in the pit of his stomach, one he'd learned a long time ago not to ignore. "We have to find her."

"We will. If we don't catch up with her on the road, we'll figure out who she's meeting with and crash their appointment. Won't be the first time we've messed up her schedule, and I doubt it'll be the last. Now get your head on straight. I knew I should've driven."

"My car, I drive." He stared through the windshield, his eyes laser focused on the road. He couldn't bear it if something happened to Serena, yet his intuition was clanging louder than a red alert on *Star Trek*.

"I'm gonna call Ridge again, see if he's caught up to her."

"He'd have called us if he had. Keep your eyes peeled."

The miles sped past as he raced toward the Big House, but it was almost an hour outside of the main part of town, if he obeyed the speed limits—which he wasn't. The urge to find her grew with each passing minute.

"Bro, slow down, there's a car blocking the road."

Antonio had already hit the brakes, because he'd seen the cars in the road. Three of them actually, and one of them was Serena's. The other belonged to his brother, Ridge, who he was climbing from the driver's side. He didn't recognize the third one.

"There's Serena's Camry."

Antonio turned his head to stare at his brother. "You think I don't recognize her car? Who's the other one belong to?"

Rafe shook his head. "I don't recognize it. Let's take a look."

While Rafe strode toward the black sedan, Antonio sprinted toward Serena's car. Ridge squatted down by the front end, examining the damage. Though his cowboy hat shaded the upper part of his face, Antonio noted his clenched jaw and unsmiling face. He stood and tried to open the driver's door, but it didn't budge.

"Looks like the sedan hit the front end, forcing her off the road. There's damage, but I'd say it's still drivable. She probably climbed out the passenger side. Door's open."

"Have you seen Serena?" Antonio scanned the blacktop and the trees lining the road, searching for signs of her. Then he peered in through the driver's window, noting the exploded airbag and powder covering the inside. He sprinted around to the passenger side, where the door hung open, and squatted down on the shoulder of the road. Covered with rocks and grass, the ground was wet and muddy from the rain earlier, and etched in the mud he noted two sets of footprints, one distinctly a male's.

"Antonio, come look at this." Rafe motioned him over to the sedan, and pointed to the street. "That's Serena's phone. Looks like somebody smashed it."

"We've got footprints by the passenger door of Serena's car. At least two sets, one of them definitely a male. Driver's door doesn't open, she must've climbed out the other side."

"But where is she? Or the driver?"

Antonio stared at his brother, his mind racing in a million directions, and none of them were good. They had to find her. He couldn't lose her, not this way. He'd made a promise to protect her—and he'd failed.

"Bro?" Ridge's voice broke the silent stare down between brothers. "Looks like footprints heading into the tree line. I'm going to take a look, see if I can find her."

"Wait for me." Antonio turned to Rafe. "You stay here. Call in the accident and get help. I have to find her."

"Go. I've got this. I'll catch up when I can."

Antonio sprinted over to where Ridge stood, close to the

live oaks so prevalent in Texas. Dead branches were scattered along the ground, blown free during the high winds and dry summer months, and piles of scattered brown crispy leaves littered the forest floor. Ridge pointed to disturbed spots in the mud, where feet had obviously tramped through.

"One smaller set, and one larger."

"Serena. The others must belong to the driver. Let's go." Antonio took off at a slow jog, trying to keep his eyes on the ground and keep from running head first into tree trunks. It was rough going after about fifty feet or so, because the trees were denser, and the ground wasn't as wet, and the footprints began disappearing.

Ridge kept pace with him. He knew his brother felt guilty Serena had left under his watch, but he was glad his brother was helping him search. Of all his brothers, Ridge was the best tracker in the bunch. If there was a trail to follow, Ridge would find it.

He kept pushing forward, Ridge close by his side, until Ridge threw an arm across Antonio's chest, stopping him in his tracks. When he looked at his brother, Ridge raised a finger to his lips, then closed his eyes. After a few seconds, he pointed to his right and began walking in that direction, his steps cautious and deliberate, trying not to make any noise. Antonio's heart was in his throat as he followed his brother's path, knowing Ridge had heard something he hadn't.

Precious seconds passed as they continued forward, but a piercing scream had Ridge racing forward, Antonio right on his heels. Serena! The scream had come from Serena. Listening as he ran, Antonio prayed like he'd never prayed before he'd reach her in time.

A muffled curse came from up ahead, this time the voice deep and decidedly masculine. Thrashing noises, along with sounds of a struggle filled the stillness. Antonio's legs burned with each racing step, his sole focus, his only goal—get to Serena. He sped past a stand of trees, spotting a man several yards away, standing over a prone body.

A blurred movement at his side, and Ridge launched himself at the male, knocking him to the ground. Antonio sprawled to his knees beside Serena's prone body. Her eyes were closed, and he could see her taking shallow breaths. Blood matted her hair and splattered across her forehead.

"Serena, sweetheart, tell me you're okay."

She didn't answer, didn't move, even as his hands slid over her body, checking for injuries. He couldn't see anything too serious, at least not to his cursory glance, but she still hadn't opened her eyes.

"Get back here, you little weasel."

He looked up at Ridge's yell, and saw a man take off running, darting in and out of the trees and bushes, headed back toward the road. Right now, he didn't care. Either Ridge would catch him, or he'd run into Rafe when he exited the tree line. All he could think about, all he cared about was Serena. She was hurt, how badly he couldn't tell, and it worried him she hadn't woken up.

Running his fingers along her scalp, he found a knot the size of a goose egg on the back of her head. No, no, no! Digging in his pocket, he pulled out his cell phone and dialed Rafe.

"Tell me EMTs are on their way."

"Should be here any minute. Did you find Serena?"

Antonio took a deep breath before answering. "Yes, but she's hurt. I can't tell how bad, but she's unconscious and has a big lump on the back of her head. There's blood on her forehead and her face. Ridge is chasing some guy, I guess he was the driver. They're headed back toward the road."

"I'll keep my eyes peeled. Where are you, so I can send the paramedics back?"

Antonio gave him basic directions and hung up. Why wouldn't she wake up? He needed to see her eyes open, have her tell him he was worrying over nothing, and she'd be fine.

Sirens in the distance told him help was only minutes away, yet each one seemed an eternity. He watched Serena's chest rise and fall with each breath, but he was afraid to move her in case she was hurt worse than he could assess. His hands itched to pull her into his arms, know she was okay, and everything would be fine.

Why aren't the paramedics here yet? I can't lose her! I can't!

The crunching of dry leaves and shuffling feet was a welcome sound, it meant help had arrived. Uniformed EMTs stepped through the trees, and he stood, taking one step back and then another, letting them come closer. Rafe strode over and stood by his side, having followed the EMTs from the road.

"You okay?"

Antonio shook his head, his eyes glued to the two men checking Serena for injuries. A cervical collar was slipped around her neck, and he winced. She looked so small and helpless lying on the dirty ground. It tore him up inside, guilt and fear a heady cocktail playing with his emotions.

"Did you see Ridge or the other guy?"

"I was busy bringing the paramedics back, had to show them where you guys were. Dusty should be here any minute, along with a tow truck to haul in the wrecks."

Antonio watched the paramedics gently lift Serena onto the backboard they'd carried into the wooded area. Bright red blood across her forehead accentuated the paleness of her skin. The dappled light through the trees cast eerie shadows, making the area dark and sinister, and he wanted her out of here. She deserved sunshine and light, not this dank, darkness covered in mud and decay.

"She's got lacerations and bruises, and a pretty bad bump on the back of her skull. Probably a concussion. I'm a little worried she hasn't regained consciousness yet. We'll transport her to the emergency clinic and have them check her out."

"I'm going with you." Antonio kept pace with the EMTs, his eyes never leaving Serena.

"I'll find out what happened and meet you there," Rafe

promised.

The EMTs made quick work of loading her into the back of the ambulance, and Antonio climbed on board and reached for her hand. The need to touch her, watch her breathe, nearly overwhelmed him. Somehow, Serena had wormed her way into his heart and mind in a way he'd never expected, and he was afraid he'd lose her. He couldn't. The thought was unbearable.

The sirens blared as they sped toward the emergency clinic, with Antonio praying the whole way. The clinic served Shiloh Springs for most non-life-threatening issues, and was closer than trying to get Serena to the hospital, which was over an hour away. Once the doctor evaluated her, if needed, they'd Medevac her. Chances were good she had a concussion and nothing more serious, like internal injuries. He squeezed her hand, his eyes never leaving her pale face, and willed her to wake up.

This had to end once and for all. Serena needed peace and safety, without the threat of Big Jim Berkley and his followers or the federal government breathing down her neck. Somehow, some way, he was going to make it happen or die trying.

CHAPTER FIFTEEN

Serena opened her eyes, wincing at the light shining through the window. She tried raising her hand to block out the glare, but couldn't move it. There was a weight keeping her from lifting it, and when she looked, she couldn't help smiling. A dark, masculine head lay cradled against her palm, the hair mussed, but she'd recognize those wavy locks anywhere.

Why was Antonio lying in a chair in her room? Only it wasn't her room, she realized, as memories started flooding back. The accident. Drury. Running for her life through the woods.

A monitor at the head of her bed beeped quietly. If she listened closely, she could heart footsteps outside the partially open door across from her bed. It didn't look like a hospital room, so it had to be the emergency clinic. Last she'd heard, Doctor Jennings was getting ready to retire and had hired a new doctor to take over running the clinic and handling the emergency situations.

"Good morning, pretty lady."

Serena smiled at Doctor Jennings. Guess he hadn't bit

the retirement bullet yet. His white coat was pristine, crisp and looked freshly pressed. A stethoscope hung around his neck, and his blue eyes sparkled with humor. He nodded toward the still sleeping Antonio.

"I hear he's been here all night. Wouldn't leave, no matter how hard the staff tried."

Antonio raised his head at the doctor's words, his eyes going to Serena. "How are you feeling?"

"I'm okay. A little sore." His brow raised at her blatant lie. "Okay, a lot sore."

"Not surprising. You got pretty banged up." Doctor Jennings strode over to her bedside, and turned to face Antonio. "You need to wait outside while I examine Miss Serena. Tell Betty Sue I'm ready for her."

"I'd rather stay." Antonio's expression turned mulish, and Serena was afraid there was going to be a confrontation between him and the doctor.

"Son, it don't matter what you want. There are rules in the clinic, and one of 'em is putting patient care first. Now, I need to take a gander at your gal, and then you can come back in. I wasn't on call when she was brought in yesterday, Doc Stevens was. He's good, but I still need to check Miss Serena myself, make sure we've got all the bases covered and she doesn't need to be transferred. Now get Betty Sue, and wait outside. The faster you leave, the faster you'll get back in here."

Antonio hesitated and Serena touched his hand. "It's

okay. Get the nurse and let them check me over, so we can go home."

"I'll be right outside. Call me if you need anything."

He spun on his heel and stormed out of the room, and Doctor Jennings gave her a wink. "He's got it bad."

Serena shook her head, instantly regretting the movement. "It's not like that. He's just a friend. There's nothing between us. He's protecting me…it's complicated."

Betty Sue, the nurse who worked the day shift at the clinic, slipped through the door and gave her a smile. He took the stethoscope from around his neck and placed the disk against her chest. "Well, if he's protecting you, I'd say he's falling down on the job."

"I wasn't supposed to leave the Big House, but I needed to meet with a client. The accident wasn't Antonio's fault."

"I'm teasing you, gal. I've known Antonio ever since he moved in with the Boudreaus. Shoot, I've patched up and stitched more cuts on that boy than I can count. He's grown into a good man." He stared at her, his expression somber. "You ain't gonna find anybody better than Antonio."

Serena felt the heat rush into her cheeks. "It's not like that. We aren't…we haven't…" Her words trailed off at the smirk on the older man's face. For an octogenarian, he was pretty darn intuitive.

"He's right," Betty Sue added. "I got here at five a.m., and he was sitting there, didn't budge when I was checking your vitals. You woke up, looked around, spotted him and went right back to sleep, like him being there made you feel better."

"From what Doc Stevens told me, Antonio ain't left your side from the moment the ambulance pulled into the driveway. Spent the night in the chair, holding your hand. Kinda hard not to think there's more than mere acquaintanceship between you two." He pulled out a penlight from his pocket. "Now, let's take a look at your head."

Serena endured the examination, all the poking and prodding. Betty Sue changed a few of her bandages, and Doctor Jennings studied the x-ray of her left wrist, before giving a final nod.

"Looks like it ain't broken, but you're going to have to keep it bandaged for stability and be in a sling for a while. It's a nasty sprain. You were lucky. With a car accident, things could have been a lot worse. You do have a concussion. You lost consciousness, and didn't come to until the EMTs got you here. We're gonna keep you here another twenty-four hours."

"But, I—"

"No buts, young lady. A concussion is nothing to play around with. No arguments, you're staying."

"Yes, sir."

"Good answer," he grinned. "Now, I'll send your fella back in, and give you a bit of privacy. Get some rest, maybe get some sleep, and tomorrow, if things look good, we'll let you go home."

"Thank you, Doctor Jennings."

"Holler if you need anything." Betty Sue headed for the door behind the doctor, and Antonio burst into the room the second it opened. Doctor Jennings shook his head and kept going. Betty Sue turned and gave her a thumb's up behind Antonio's back, and Serena bit back her laugh.

"You okay?"

"Yes, although they're going to make me stay another twenty-four hours."

He slid onto the seat he'd vacated earlier and reached for her right hand. "Not a bad idea. You were out for a long time."

"That's what Doctor Jennings said."

"How much do you remember about the accident?"

She leaned back against the pillows and tried to piece together everything that had happened. "I got a call from a client."

"Yeah, I read the note you left. What were you thinking, Serena? I thought you understood somebody had to be with you at all times if you left the Big House. Why do you think Ridge was there?"

She gave a long, drawn-out sigh, awash with guilt. "I know. I feel so stupid. When Mr. Olson called, I thought I'd only be gone for a little while. Show him a property and come right back. He's been a client ever since I moved here, and he's been trying to get a look at this property for a year at least, maybe longer. I didn't want to disappoint him."

"And you couldn't take two minutes to call Ridge in from the barn?" Antonio's voice held an edge to it, one he'd never directed at her before. She'd honestly disappointed him, and something inside her cringed at how horrible it made her feel.

"I didn't think, okay?"

"We'll get back to that. Tell me what you remember about the accident."

She closed her eyes, picturing again the car speeding toward her, and swerving into her lane, feeling the jolt of the impact, and the airbag deploying. She detailed everything to him. "Everything happened so fast, it's almost a blur. I couldn't get out of the car on the driver's side, and had to crawl across and get out on the passenger side."

"We saw when we got to the scene." Serena wondered what he felt when he'd seen her car at the side of the road. Had he worried about her? Right now, he seemed so detached, and she couldn't tell if it was because he was in professional mode, wanting all the facts, or if he didn't care. She'd thought they were getting closer, but maybe she'd read too much into things, and her feelings were all one-sided, and he really didn't want anything more than to be friends.

"Anyway," she continued, wanting to get through with this, "I went to the other car to see if they needed help. The driver was hunched over the steering wheel, and didn't respond when I tapped on the passenger window."

"Why didn't you call for help?"

"I did—well, I mean, I started to, but he pulled a gun and told me to toss my phone on the ground."

Antonio leaned in closer, his intent stare boring into her like a laser, focused and unreadable. "What happened next?"

"He got out of the car and stomped on my phone. Twice."

"Did you recognize the driver, Serena?"

She nodded, her fingers picking at the satin edging of the blanket covering her. "Yes. I wasn't sure at first, when he was slumped over the wheel, but once he turned toward me, there was no doubt."

"Who?"

"Jonathan Drury, my uncle's attorney."

Antonio's brow rose at the name, and he pulled out his cellphone and began typing, then laid the phone on the mattress. "Go on."

"It was weird. He talked about my being his ticket out. Said my uncle was crazy, and he needed to get away from him. None of it made any sense." She didn't want to say the next part, but knew Antonio would get it out of her anyway. Might as well bite the bullet and say it. "He said my uncle knows where I am, and he's put a hit out on me."

Antonio leaned his head back and stared at the ceiling, and exhaled a deep breath. "We kinda saw it coming. I checked with Rafe earlier, and there weren't any fingerprints in your townhouse, no fibers, nothing to show anybody was there." When she started to speak, he held up his hand. "I believe you. Somebody was there, they're just good at covering their tracks. A pro."

Serena wanted to throw up. She'd been so careful, hiding in plain sight, and now everything had crumbled into a pile of ashes. Jonathan showing up hadn't been a coincidence; her uncle *knew* she was in Shiloh Springs. Her hands gripped the edge of the blanket until her knuckles turned white.

"Antonio, I have to leave."

"No, sweetheart, you're not going anywhere. No more running or hiding. Rafe's going to have somebody outside your door until the doctor releases you. I'm going to talk with Williamson today. He's going to want to talk to you too."

"I can't believe I'm going to have to go through all this again. I wish…"

"Big Jim is still behind bars, and he's going to stay there until his appeal goes before the judge. In the meantime, we'll fight to come up with something to keep him there. I'm going to talk to Drury."

Serena rubbed her forehead, the dull throbbing pain intensifying into a full-blown headache. "Don't let him fool you. He seems laid back and disarming, but it's all an act. A façade he's honed to perfection through the years. He comes across as an Average Joe, but the man is a shark in the courtroom. And my uncle pulls his strings like a master puppeteer. If Big Jim says jump, Jonathan will be hopping before he even asks how high."

"Shh. Let me do my job, I'm pretty good at it. In the meantime, you rest, and do what the doctor tells you."

Serena closed her eyes, blinking back the tears threatening to spill. "Antonio, I'm scared."

He stood, moving closer until he was by the head of the bed. She felt his lips brush against her forehead in a gentle kiss. Such a simple sign of affection, but it unleashed the waterworks, the tears flowing down her cheeks, great, gulping sobs wracking her body. Antonio sat on the edge of the bed and pulled her into his arms, cradling her against his chest, his strength like a bulwark against the world.

All the pent-up rage, despair, and anxiety unleashed in a barrage of tears, and she wrapped her good arm around him, needing the feel of his embrace like a lifeline, the single constant she could latch onto as a tsunami of feelings flooded her, crashing through her with the ferocity of a tidal wave. One hand cradled her head against his chest, while the other moved in soothing strokes along her spine, as her sobs devolved into teary hiccups.

When the torrent began abating, he leaned back and stared into her eyes, studying her with an intensity which shocked and thrilled her in equal measure. It felt like he could see clear to the depths of her soul. She felt raw and exposed beneath his perusal, flayed open to reveal every secret, every hope and desire. When his hand cupped her cheek, she leaned into his touch, trusting him not to abuse the trust she was putting in him. She'd been hurt so many times in the past, betrayed and used. With Antonio, she prayed for a new start. A tiny kernel, if tended and nurtured, might grow into something—wonderful.

"I promise I won't let anything happen to you. You're safe now, and I intend to make sure you stay that way." His thumb stroked across her cheek, the touch light and gentle. "It's too soon, I know, but I...care about you."

Serena's eyes widened at his words, but even more at the emotion behind them. Did he mean what she thought he did, or was she reading too much into the statement? Deciding to throw what little pride and dignity she had left to the winds, she blurted out, "Antonio, I...I care about you too." She changed what she'd started to say at the last moment. Saying those three little words shouldn't be so hard, but she'd never said them to anybody before, and was terrified he didn't return her feelings. It was too soon and she was still feeling exposed, filleted to the bone, with all the revelations over the last couple of days.

"When I get back, you and I are going to talk. No more hiding and no excuses. Got it?"

She swallowed past the lump in her throat. "Got it. Antonio, please be careful."

"Don't worry about me, sweetheart. Drury's not going to hurt me, and I'm going to find out exactly what he knows, and what Big Jim's plans are. This will all be over soon, I promise."

"I can't help worrying. You don't know my uncle like I

do. He's dangerous. Just because he's behind bars doesn't mean he's incompetent or impotent. He still yields a lot of power. It's honestly been a miracle I've stayed off his radar this long."

"Well, you've got a whole lot of people looking out for you now, and we're not going to let anything happen to you. Now, you do what you're told and I'll be back, depending on how things go with Drury."

"Call me after you talk to him?"

He smiled, and touched her nose with the tip of his finger. "I will. Get some rest." He reached forward and brushed a strand of hair behind her ear. "Even if it wasn't my job, I'd still watch over you. Keep you safe. I'll do everything in my power to never let you get hurt again, Serena. Haven't you figured out how much I care about you? Seeing you here, knowing I wasn't there when you needed me the most, it's tearing me up inside."

"Antonio, stop. None of this is your fault." Her brown eyes stared at him, damp with unshed tears.

"Then let me take care of you. Before you say anything else, I know you aren't helpless, just the opposite. You've done a magnificent job of keeping yourself safe for a long time with nobody's help. You are smart and savvy and independent, and know how to do things nobody else can. It's different this time, because you aren't alone. You've got so many friends in Shiloh Springs, more than you can imagine. You've got Momma and Dad, and all my pain in the backside, overprotective brothers. And you've got me."

Serena weighed each word, letting them sink in, and she finally gave a watery smile. "Alright. I'll let you wrap me in bubble wrap and sock me away at the Big House this one time, if you'll promise me you'll be careful. You don't know the people you're dealing with, but I do. Big Jim, Drury, they're not going to stop until I'm no longer a threat."

"Then I'll have to make sure they don't have a reason to come after you."

Leaning over her prone form, he stared down into her face, and she stared back, memorizing every inch, committing to memory his dark hair, eyes that seemed to see straight through to her soul, and yet didn't find her wanting. Every time she saw him, whenever he'd been in Shiloh Springs, watching him around his family, made her want him more. Being this close to him made her breathless, giddy, and infatuated with a fire she didn't think would ever be quenched.

When her lips parted slightly, her tiny pink tongue sweeping along the plump bottom one, she gave in to impulse and cupped the back of his head, pulling him in and pressing her lips against his, tasting the intoxicating sweetness of his kiss. Felt his tentative response as her lips brushed against his. He deepened the kiss, and she felt a tingle of sensation at the brush of his mouth against hers. Barely noticed when her fingers threaded through his hair. As much as she wanted to take things farther, deeper, now wasn't the time or the place.

Reluctantly, she pulled back with one last sip at his lips, breathing in his intoxicating scent, and gave a rueful smile. When she started to lower her hand from where the fingers had been tangled in his hair, he caught it, placed a gentle kiss against her palm, and folded her fingers inward, as if to capture the kiss and hold it forever.

After what seemed far too brief a time, he pulled back, his eyes searching her face before he straightened to his full height and took a step back. "I really have to go. Rafe's got one of his deputies posted outside, if you need anything."

With a last lingering look, he turned and walked out the door. Serena's fingertips traced her lips, still feeling the tingle from their kiss. Drawing in a deep breath, she laid back against the pillows.

"I am in so much trouble."

CHAPTER SIXTEEN

Antonio knocked on the front door and glanced around, surveilling his surroundings. He'd made the long drive from Shiloh Springs to Oklahoma City, the entire way marked by construction and detours. US 75, normally a nightmare to drive on the best of days, especially going through downtown Dallas, today had been almost impassable. The whole trip ended up taking him two hours longer than anticipated, and he was tired, cranky, and he really hoped Jonathon Drury didn't give him an excuse to lose his temper.

He'd left Serena in the hospital, bruised and scraped, with her sprained wrist bandaged, after her run in with Drury. So he was running on coffee, adrenaline, and anger, not a good combination when questioning a suspect. While he hadn't seen Drury attack Serena with his own eyes, he had no doubt Drury had been behind running Serena off the road and chasing her through the woods with a gun. Balling his hands into fists, he fought to control his temper. He had to keep his cool, do everything by the book. Drury was smart, as evidenced by his manipulating the judicial system to get Big Jim Berkley a new trial. He couldn't afford to underestimate his quarry, but he planned to make sure one way or another Drury didn't get away with hurting Serena.

The front door swung inward, and a heavy-set woman stood in the opening, a perturbed scowl on her face. Oily, dark hair hung limply around her face, and glasses with thick tortoise shell rims covered a good portion of her face. Somehow, she didn't resemble the picture he had of a successful attorney's wife. Instead, she looked more like— well, he wasn't going to go there. She looked as unhappy to see him at her door as he was to be there, but he had a job to do, and he wasn't leaving without answers. If he wasn't happy with what he learned, Drury would be in handcuffs, headed for the police station.

"Mrs. Drury?"

"Yeah. Can I help you?" Her gaze swept over him from the top of his head to his toes, and back up again, and she blinked a couple of times before plastering a smile on her lips.

Antonio pasted an answering smile on his face and turned on the charm, burying his seething anger down. He hoped a little kindness might loosen Mrs. Drury's lips, get her talking, and if he was lucky, she'd implicate her husband in Serena's accident.

"My name is Antonio Boudreau. FBI." He pulled his shield, showing her his identification. Watched her eyes widen in surprise. "I'd like to speak with you and your husband. May I come in?"

"I guess so."

Oh, boy, she doesn't sound like a happy camper.

She led him into the living room, and he couldn't hide his surprise. From the outside, the house didn't appear to be more than a modest ranch style in an upper middle-class neighborhood. Inside, it looked like the Liberace Museum vomited all over the living room. Shiny brass, silver, and glittering crystals covered every surface. An explosion of pink in every shade imaginable assaulted his eyes. Zebra print sofas sat pushed back against two walls. Armchairs with scrolled arms covered with gold velvet and crystal-studded nail head trim anchored the corners. A blinding hot pink rug lay centered between all the furniture, and mirrored glass end-tables flanked the sofas. He found himself rendered speechless from the overabundance of bad taste and extravagance crowding the space.

Mrs. Drury sat primly on the edge of one of the sofas, her hands folded demurely in her lap. She presented an incongruous sight, with her mousy brown hair which looked like it could use a good shampooing, and tortoise shell, thick-lensed glasses. The huge bright orange and violet flowers on her blouse clashed with the zebra print, and her yellow capri pants practically burned his corneas.

"Mrs. Drury—"

"Please, call me Corinne." She gave him a shy smile, her words a bit flirtatious, and battered her lashes at him. Or maybe she was having trouble with her vision, he couldn't tell because of the thick glasses. Didn't matter, he couldn't afford to let his surroundings or her odd behavior distract him from getting the answers he needed. The plan was to ease into the conversation, get her talking, and prove Drury didn't have an alibi for the time he'd been in Shiloh Springs. Thinking back to Serena's poor bruised and battered body had his hands fisting. But he needed to keep it together and let Mrs. Drury confirm his suspicions.

They'd found Serena's stolen car over an hour away from Shiloh Springs, abandoned in a shopping center parking lot. Drury had taken it, making his getaway while Rafe and Antonio had been rescuing Serena in the woods. Though Ridge had chased after Drury, he'd lost him in heavy traffic outside Austin. Currently the car was being gone over with a fine-tooth comb, the FBI crime techs searching for finger-prints, fibers, or anything else to prove Drury drove it, because the only person who'd gotten a good look at him after the accident was Serena. All Ridge could tell was the man running away was approximately the right height and build for Drury, but he hadn't gotten a good look at his face.

"Corinne, is Mr. Drury home? I'd like to ask him some questions as well."

"Jonathan isn't due back for a while, Mr. Boudreau." She coquettishly curled a clump of oily hair around her finger, and gave him another simpering smile, which didn't do anything except turn his stomach. Was she seriously trying to flirt with him? He needed to get her focused and answering questions, and made an effort to get her attention off him and back onto her husband.

"I see. Well, I do have a couple of questions you might be able to answer. Where was your husband yesterday?"

The hair-twirling finger stopped mid-twirl and she sat a little straighter. "He was here at home. Why?"

"Was he here all day, Mrs. Drury? Did he leave at any time?"

"What is this about, Mr. Boudreau? My husband hasn't done anything wrong."

"I'm following up on an accident. Looking for potential witnesses. You understand." Antonio didn't want to come right out and tell *Corinne* he wanted to toss her husband under the jail for hurting Serena. Or that FBI agents didn't normally go around looking for eyewitnesses to car accidents. That was handled by the local cops.

"You think he saw an accident? Oh, I don't think so. He was here—"

The front door swung open hard enough to bang against the wall, and Drury raced inside, red-faced and out of breath. His eyes frantically scanned the room before spotting Antonio. In a surprising move, Jonathan stalked across the room and got right up in Antonio's face, his anger an almost palpable thing.

"Why are you bothering my wife?" He slung an arm around Corinne, pulling her against his side. She slid both arms around Drury's waist and rested her head against his chest, hugging him close.

"Honey, it's okay. He's with the FBI. He wants to talk to you about an accident."

Drury ran a gentle hand over his wife's head before cupping her cheek. "I'm sure it's a mistake. I don't know anything about an accident. I'm afraid I can't help you, Mr. Boudreau."

The tiny hairs of the back of Antonio's neck tingled at the mention of his name. Neither he nor Drury's wife had mentioned him by name, simply he was with the FBI. Somebody must have snitched to Drury about a stranger showing up at his house. The neighborhood grapevine moved quickly when it wanted to and small-town suburbs, like this one, meant neighbors watched out for each other. Guess somebody must've called Drury when they'd seen Antonio show up on his doorstep. Didn't explain how he'd known Antonio's name, but it did mean Drury knew a whole lot more than Antonio expected. Apparently Big Jim's mouthpiece was neck deep in his conspiracy and his attempt on Serena's life.

"Mr. Drury, where were you yesterday?"

Drury glanced at his wife before answering. "Here. All day. I never left the house."

Antonio watched the imperceptible stiffening of Corinne's body at Drury's lie, but she didn't contradict him. "Can anybody confirm your story?"

"Of course. My wife can. Right, sweetie?"

"That's what I was telling Mr. Boudreau. You were home all day. With me."

"I have witnesses who claim you were in Texas yesterday, Mr. Drury. And you were involved in an automobile accident with another car. Are you denying their account?"

Drury nodded. "Absolutely. Whoever told you that is either mistaken or a bald-faced liar. I emphatically deny being in Texas or anywhere else yesterday, except for right here, in my home." He paused, defiantly staring at Antonio. "Am I being accused of anything, Mr. Boudreau? I have to assume it's serious, if they've sent the Federal Bureau of Investigation to interrogate me."

"Mr. Drury, this is not an interrogation, it's an informal inquiry into an accident and attempted kidnapping in Central Texas. I'm sure you understand the gravity of the situation. We have to cover all angles and investigate any facts to determine the guilty parties involved."

"Kidnapping? Now you've definitely piqued my interest. Who'd they attempt to snatch?"

The smirk on Drury's face made Antonio's hand itch to slap it right off his smug face. With his wife corroborating his alibi, Drury knew Antonio couldn't touch him. Yet. He'd have to sit tight and wait for the evidence from the car search. SAC Williamson was having somebody check with the car rental agency to see if they could get a description of the person who'd rented the sedan, but until then, he was stuck between a rock and a hard place.

"I'm afraid that's privileged information. Do you have any idea why someone would want to implicate you in this situation?"

"I'm afraid not."

"What about Big Jim Berkley's case? I heard he's eligible for a new trial thanks to you. Congratulations." It left a nasty taste in his mouth, saying those words, but he needed to make the little weasel think he was off the hook, even if only temporarily. "Any chance this could be related?"

Drury seemed to think about his question for a moment. "Doubtful. It wasn't announced until yesterday, so nobody outside of the Department of Justice was aware of the reversal of the previous decision. Afraid I can't think of a single reason why somebody would think I'd be involved, Mr. Boudreau."

"Well, I had to ask. Cover all the bases, you understand. Mrs. Drury, were you at home all day yesterday as well?"

Corinne nodded, her arms still wrapped around her husband's waist. She hadn't torn herself from his side since the moment he'd rocketed through the door. Antonio didn't belief for one nanosecond either was telling the truth, but without any corroborating evidence, he had to walk away. But this wasn't over, not by a long shot. He'd have Drury in handcuffs for what he did to Serena, and it looked like his wife might be right by his side in a jail cell for perjury.

"You've answered all the questions I have at this time."

He pulled a card from his pocket and handed it to Drury. "If you think of anything, give me a call. I'd like to get this case settled and find out who's behind the attempted kidnapping."

Drury took the card and shoved it into his pocket. "We'll will."

Antonio gave Drury one final look, reading the satisfaction in the other man's eyes. He honestly thought he'd gotten away with trying to abduct Serena. Let him believe that, because his days as a free man were numbered.

It was a promise.

CHAPTER SEVENTEEN

Serena elevated the bed higher so she was partially sitting up. Flipping through the channels on the TV wasn't helping. She couldn't stop thinking about Antonio. He'd kissed her! Did it mean something more than a simple kiss or was she reading way too much into the simple gesture?

A quiet knock on the door drew her thoughts away from the kiss to the man standing inside her room. He was tall, with sandy brown hair and a pair of sunglasses covering his eyes. A Stetson in his hand, along with his formal bearing, told her more than words he was some kind of fed. Either FBI or maybe Texas Rangers, but he was definitely government.

"Ms. Berkley?"

"I'm sorry, but no, I'm Serena Snowden."

He walked further into the room and closed the door quietly behind him. When he pulled off the sunglasses, his startling green eyes speared her, telling her he saw straight through her lie. "I'm Derrick Williamson, FBI. I'm the Special Agent in Charge from the Austin office. I'd like to talk to you about your uncle, James Berkley."

"I told you—"

"Don't bother to lie, I have all the proof I need to know you are Sharon Berkley, but if it makes you more comfortable, I'll call you Ms. Snowden."

Serena threw her hands up. "Fine, call me whatever you want. You obviously know everything."

He pulled a chair up beside the bed and eased his lanky frame onto the seat. "How are you doing? I heard about the accident."

"Antonio called you?"

Williamson shook his head, a lock of hair falling across his forehead. It gave him a younger, more approachable look. "I was already on my way here. Antonio and Rafe convinced me to let the Boudreaus protect you at their ranch. I agreed, since they assured me you'd be safer there than in witness protection."

"Oh." Guilt speared through her, remembering how she'd disobeyed the one thing Antonio asked, and left the ranch without taking anybody with her. It was her fault he was in trouble, and she couldn't let him take the rap. "Antonio's not to blame. I'm the one who didn't listen, who left the ranch without backup. He's not responsible."

She watched Williamson's lips turn up at the corners, but couldn't tell what he was thinking. He was a hard man to read. "Ms. Snowden, Mr. Boudreau isn't in trouble. He's doing his job, like I'm doing mine. Which is why I'm here on a Sunday, instead of at home with my son, watching football."

"I'm sorry."

"There's enough blame to go around. I have to admit, I admire your ability to stay off the grid and under the government's radar. Not a lot of people can. I'm impressed."

"It wasn't like I had a lot of choice," Serena mumbled under her breath.

"You're right." Her head jerked up at his response. He'd heard her muttered comment, and she felt heat rush into her face. "Witness protection failed you not once, but twice, and for that you have my sincerest apologies. I've been assured the party who leaked your information to an outside source is now spending quality time behind bars. But I'm a skeptical man by nature, and like Boudreau, I can't be one hundred percent confident all the holes have been plugged, which is why I agreed to his proposal for you to stay at his parents' ranch."

"And I pulled a rookie stunt and blew everything to smithereens."

"I'm hopeful we can salvage things. Can you tell me about your accident? How much do you remember?"

"I went over all this with Antonio and again with Rafe."

Williamson nodded. "I know, and I've got copies of their reports, but I'd like to hear your version. Now some time has passed, maybe you'll remember something you didn't before. Let's start from the beginning."

Serena told him exactly what she'd told Antonio and

Rafe, about getting the phone call from Mr. Olson and heading out to meet him. Explained how she'd been hit by the car and pushed off the road. The shock at finding out her uncle's lawyer, Jonathan Drury, was the driver of the other car. Williamson listened intently, not interrupting, which was a rarity because both Rafe and Antonio had stopped her throughout the retelling with a myriad of questions.

"You mentioned Drury said you were his ticket to freedom. Any idea what he meant?"

"Not a clue, but that's what he said. I was his ticket to freedom and he was going to cash it in."

Williamson leaned back in the chair, and stared out the window, not saying a word. Serena wondered what she'd said, because it was like he was turning something over in his mind, putting all the puzzle pieces together. Maybe he'd be able to figure out something from Drury's odd comments. She'd wracked her brain for the answer, and all she'd come up with was Drury holding her for ransom and blackmailing her uncle. She knew that wouldn't work. Big Jim would as soon kill him as pay him, and Drury should know he'd never get away with trying to bamboozle Big Jim Berkley.

"Mr. Williamson?"

His attention snapped back to her. "Sorry, toying with a couple of ideas I need to check. Is there anything you need, Ms. Snowden?"

"Call me Serena. What's going to happen now? Am I going to Austin or D.C.?"

A brief smile tugged at his lips and was gone so fast, Serena wasn't positive she'd actually seen it. He stood and picked up his hat, placing it atop his head and pulled his sunglasses out of his pocket.

"I think you need to stay exactly where you are, Serena. Boudreau can take you back to his family's ranch once the docs discharge you. The sheriff assures me he's got officers lining up for bodyguard duty, and I'm going to make sure we've got a couple of FBI agents here as well."

The knot in the middle of Serena's chest loosened, and she felt like she could breathe again. "Thank you."

"I know it's got to be hard, knowing your uncle is getting another trial and you're probably going to have to testify again. For what it's worth, I think you're an extremely brave young lady."

Serena huffed out a laugh. "Funny, I don't feel brave."

Williamson pulled a card out of his pocket, wrote something on the back, and handed it to Serena. "My personal cell number is on the back. If you need me for anything—*anything*—call me. I can be here in less than two hours."

"Thanks." She tapped the card against her bandaged hand. "Can I ask you something?"

"Of course."

"How long do you think it's going to be before my uncle goes to court? I don't want to impose on the Boudreaus for any longer than needed."

At her words, Williamson chuckled. "I doubt they look

on you as a burden. Especially Antonio. As for your question, the DOJ is pushing for an early date. But, and this is only speculation on my part, if Drury is up to his neck in behind-the-scenes machinations, like your accident, it could push the date back by several months. Possibly years."

She leaned back against the pillow, grimacing. "Great. My life is never going to get back to normal, is it?"

"It will. I promise." He started for the door. "I'll call you or Antonio as soon as I hear anything. Get some rest, and this time stay put."

She watched him close the door behind him, leaving her to wonder if her life could get any suckier. As much as she loved Douglas and Ms. Patti, she couldn't live with them for months, much less years.

It was time to bring out the big guns. The one secret her uncle thought nobody knew. Too bad she knew, and she had enough dirt for the Great State of Texas put a needle in his arm.

She didn't intend to fold and walk away. Not this time. She had the winning hand, and intended to play it. Picking up the phone, she started dialing.

Serena listened to the ringing on the other end of the phone, half hoping nobody answered. This was the day she'd dreaded, knowing deep in her gut, she'd one day make this call. Even with everything she'd been through—Big Jim's trial, witness protection, and being on the run—she'd always held something back, because once it became known, the life she'd built in Shiloh Springs would be over.

"Hello?" The male voice on the other end of the phone sounded like she'd woke them. A quick glance at the clock, and she winced, having forgotten the time difference. Viktor worked odd shifts, and usually slept during the afternoons. He'd probably only been asleep for a couple of hours.

"Sorry, Viktor, I forgot about the time difference."

"Sharon? Girlfriend, is that you?"

She gave a shaky laugh. "Yeah. Long time, right?"

"I haven't heard from you in over two years. Means something bad happened, right?"

"You might say that. He found me."

A vicious string of curses followed her words, and she eased the phone away from her ear, silently waiting for Viktor's rant to end. Viktor knew exactly what it meant for Big Jim to have found her, since he'd been one of the men instrumental in helping her escape from his clutches more than once, after the last time relocating to Alaska, to be as far away from Big Jim as possible and still be in the States.

"You finished?"

His gruff growl was answer enough. "What happened? Besides somebody screwing up, that is."

"It's too long a story to go into right now, and I've got a concussion, so if I sound kinda loopy, that's why."

"Concussion? He hurt you? Son of a—"

"Stop! He didn't do it, not personally. Jonathan Drury ran me off the road and then I hit my head. Like I said, I don't have time for all the details now. I'll explain everything when I can. I need…" She trailed off, knowing what she asked for next would change everything, because the information she'd kept hidden spelled disaster not only for Big Jim, but for her.

"Sharon. You okay, girl? Tell me where you are and I'll be on the next plane."

"No, don't. I—I need you to get something for me, though." She hated asking Viktor to do what she couldn't. Being stuck here in the clinic, with an FBI guard, severely limited her options, and she was down to her last one.

"Anything. You know you can ask me anything and you've got it." The affection in Viktor's voice was unmistakable, and she felt it wrap around her like a snuggly blanket she wanted to burrow beneath and never come out. That was impossible now. Big Jim had gone too far. While she was afraid for herself, all she could think about was her uncle going after the man she loved. She'd do anything to protect him.

"I need you to get something for me. Something I hid when I went into witness protection."

"I'm assuming since you're calling me, contacting the government is out of the question?"

"I kind of ran away from them after my neighbor was killed when my uncle's men found me the first time."

Another string of curses echoed over the phone. She smiled at Viktor's colorful use of language. She'd forgotten how much he cussed when he got upset, and he'd definitely learned some new words since the last time they'd spoken. Funny, even though she rarely cursed herself, she'd sort of missed Viktor's outrageous turn of phrase.

"Stop. I don't have much time." She lowered her voice to a whisper, even though the guard stood outside her partially-open door. "Do you remember the picture I gave you before the trial? The framed one of you and me?"

"Of course. It's sitting on my dresser right now." Viktor's voice was tinged with curiosity, and a little bit of why-in-the-world-are-you-asking-me-about-a-picture.

Breathing out a sigh of relief, Serena rubbed at her forehead with one hand, the headache she'd been fighting roaring in with an unexpected fierceness. She needed to ask the nurse for some pain medication, but it would have to wait until she finished her call. This was too important now, she was too close to taking down Big Jim.

"Get it. Please."

"Okay, hold on a sec." She heard the bedsprings squeaking, and Viktor's grumbling the whole time, until he came back on the line. "Now what?"

"Sorry, but you're going to have to bust the frame. In the bottom piece, there's a small thumb drive."

"Wait, what? You're kidding me. Alright, hang on, I have to put down the phone, because I need two hands."

The silence on the other end seemed to last an eternity, even though it was mere seconds. She caught herself chewing on her thumbnail, and thrust it under the blanket. Darn it, she'd broken that habit years ago, and didn't need to start again.

"Got it. What ya want me to do with it?" Viktor paused and then his voice grew louder. "Don't tell me this has something to do with your uncle on it? Sharon, I swear, have you lost your mind?"

"Viktor, I needed insurance. If for any reason my uncle had gotten off, I needed leverage with the feds, something big enough that my uncle couldn't sweep it under the table, or use his influence to get out from under. That drive is the only thing I have left, and it's enough to keep him behind bars for a very long time."

"I don't get it. He's already behind bars, isn't he?"

"His lawyers have gotten him an appeal. I—I can't let that happen. He's a monster, and he's hurt too many people. He's still hurting people. My uncle's reign of terror ends now."

Viktor sighed. "What do I do with your thumb drive?"

Serena glanced at the doorway before answering. "I need you to fly to Texas as soon as you can. Whatever it takes. Get to Austin. Take that drive to the FBI, and give it to Special Agent in Charge Derrick Williamson. Nobody else. Promise me, Viktor. Promise me you won't even look at it. Guard it with your life, because that's the only copy I have, and if anything happens to it, Big Jim will crucify me."

"Whatever this is, you're sure it's enough to take him

down for good?"

Serena felt a tingle sweep down her spine, remembering the videotape contained on the hard drive, the one she'd risked everything to make. "I'm sure."

"Alright, I'm going to catch the next flight I can get to Texas. Derrick Williamson, that's who you said?"

"Yes. I trust him. Tell him—tell him I trust him to do the right thing with it."

"Okay, you've got my word. I want this over—for you and for me. I'm still looking over my shoulder, waiting for somebody from Berkley's group to catch up with me. If he even suspected that I'm the one who fed you information, he'd have a bounty on my head faster before I could turn around. I'm scared and feel stupid because I actually believed all the snake oil he pedaled as gospel."

"A whole lot of people did, Viktor. But you helped take him down once, and getting that thumb drive to Agent Williamson will be the final nail in Big Jim's coffin. You're a good friend. I've missed you so much."

Viktor cleared his throat, the sound audible though he tried to muffle it quickly. "You too. Okay, I'm going to get a flight scheduled and get my butt to Austin. Love you, girlfriend."

"Love you too, Viktor."

With a softly whispered goodbye, she hung up the phone and prayed Viktor got the information to Williamson, and that she wasn't making the biggest mistake of her life.

CHAPTER EIGHTEEN

"Hey, Rafe, find out anything about the rental car?" Antonio tapped his fingertips on the steering while, while he inched along in traffic.

"Not much. It was rented out of Dallas under the name Sharon Berkley. Of course, the name and address are fake. The photocopy of the driver's license is such poor quality, the picture's useless. The company is sending me security camera footage, but I haven't got it yet. There are dozens of fingerprints all over the car. Should have something there soon. Serena said Drury wasn't wearing gloves, so his prints have got to be there. How'd it go on your end?"

"Lousy. Drury's wife alibis him for the entire time. Of course, she's lying through her teeth, but until I've got more than her word, I can't place him anywhere near the scene. We need those fingerprints. Thought I might have a chance to break the wife, but barely got started before everything went sideways. Funny, he showed up right after I started talking to her. My gut says somebody tipped him off. He showed up and immediately asserted his innocence, claimed to know nothing about any accident or attempted kidnapping. And the good wife backed up his story."

Antonio slowed as the construction alert flashing arrow on the interstate directed traffic over, narrowing down to one line. The construction, on top of not breaking down Drury's alibi, kept his temper bubbling just beneath the surface. He hit the horn when an idiot in a Mercedes swerved in front of him at the last second, merging into the congested highway. Good thing his weapon was in the glove box, or he might've been sorely tempted to do a little target practice on the idiot's tires.

"How's Serena?"

"Doc Stevens says she's good. They ran a couple more tests, and if she doesn't have any problems, they'll spring her first thing in the a.m."

Antonio breathed a sigh of relief. He hated seeing her lying in the clinic's bed, pale and bloody. When she'd finally opened her eyes, his whole world righted itself, where before it felt upside down and inside out. The entire ride in the back of the ambulance to the clinic, he'd prayed, begging for God to grant him a miracle and heal her, and his prayers had been answered.

"Williamson dropped by and talked to Serena," Rafe added, his tone smug. "Gotta say, he wasn't what I pictured. I thought all you FBI guys wore suits and ties, and acted all snooty."

"Bite me."

His brother's laughter proved he'd taken his comeback in

fun. "Seriously though, he seems to have a good head on his shoulders. Said he talked with Serena, and she mentioned something Drury said at the scene."

"What?"

"Serena was his ticket to freedom and he meant to cash it in. Any idea what he meant?"

Antonio thought about the words. "Not a clue. You?"

"Nope. I've been reading up on the trial. Serena's testimony was definitely the lynchpin to putting Berkley away. Without her testimony and the evidence she provided, he'd still be out instilling fear with his reign of terror."

"Drury's got several lawyers working with him on Big Jim's case, but he's the only one who's personally visited Berkley in prison. Not unusual, I guess, but there's something about this whole scenario that seems off. It stinks like rotten fish."

Traffic stopped dead, cars idling in place, and Antonio was sorely tempted to get off the freeway and drive the service roads, but that would take just as long as inching along in bumper-to-bumper congestion, even with the sporadic stops and starts. He looked up at the beep of another incoming call, the screen showing an unknown number.

"Bro, I've got another call. Let me call you back."

"No problem."

Disconnecting from Rafe, he swiped to accept the other call, hoping it wasn't some telemarketer who'd regret calling him. He was in the mood to tear somebody up one side and down the other, metaphorically speaking.

"Hello."

"Is this Antonio Boudreau?" The voice was distorted and tinny-sounding, obviously filtered through a synthesizer of some sort. Who'd want to disguise their voice?

"Yes, who's this?"

"I have information, dirt you'll find very informative, on a case you're working."

Antonio sat straighter in his seat, his curiosity piqued. "What kind of information?"

"Answer a question for me, and I'll give you everything you need."

Great, another whack job. Wonder how he got my number?

"I'll bite. What's the question?"

"How's Sharon?"

Antonio slammed on the brakes, barely missing rear-ending the car in front of him. "What did you say?"

"I know you've found her. Tell me she's alright."

"Who is this?" The command in his voice was absolute. He wasn't going to tell whoever this was a thing about Serena, but he couldn't help wondering how the caller knew he'd found her.

"I'm not an idiot, Mr. Boudreau. I know you're in your car, so you can't trace the call easily, and by the time you do, I'll be long gone. I'm not stupid enough to stay on the line long anyway. This phone will be destroyed after I hang up, so don't bother trying to find me. It's a simple quid pro quo. Answer my question, and I'll tell you where you can find enough dirt to keep Big Jim Berkley in prison, and ruin any chance he has for his upcoming appeal."

Could he risk it? He didn't have time to come up with a ploy, some way to keep the mysterious caller on the line. Out of options, he did the only thing he could.

"Sharon's fine."

"Mr. Boudreau, I know about the accident. How badly was she hurt?"

Antonio's heartbeat sped up at the caller's revelation. How could they know? Nobody outside of Shiloh Springs, except Williamson, knew they'd even found Serena, much less about the car accident. Unless the caller was Drury. It was the only explanation. Maybe he wanted the information so he could come back and finish what he'd started.

"I said she's okay. She's got a mild concussion, some cuts and bruises."

"She'll fully recover?"

"That's right."

Antonio heard a soft sigh over the speaker. It almost sounded like the caller was relieved, which would rule out Drury. Except Drury hadn't wanted Serena dead. He'd said she was his ticket to freedom. If she died, he couldn't use her for whatever he'd intended.

"You sound concerned. Do you know Sharon?"

There was a moment's hesitation. "I do—did—a long

time ago. I was glad when she got away from…all her family's mess." Antonio struggled to hear, as the call signal began cutting in and out. *Not now! I have to find out who this is and what they know.*

"If you care about her, tell me what you know. Help me keep her safe."

"I'm texting you information for a safe deposit box. I'm also overnighting a notarized authorization to access the box, as well as the key. Inside, you'll find what I promised."

"Wait—"

Before he could say another word, the call disconnected. Antonio slammed his hand against the steering wheel, frustrated he hadn't gotten more from the unidentified caller. Seconds later, the text alert dinged, again from the mystery caller. It gave the name of a bank in Dallas and the number to the safe deposit box. There was also a tracking number from an overnight courier. Strangely enough, the address the package was addressed to was the Shiloh Springs Sheriff's office. Antonio chucked at the irony.

He dialed his brother. "Want to hear something strange?"

Rafe laughed. "Lately, has there been anything not strange, bro?"

"I got a call from an unknown number. They wanted to know if *Sharon* was okay."

"Wait…what? How'd they even know we'd found her?"

"They wouldn't answer, but the caller said they had

enough information to keep Big Jim in prison for good, and avoid having to go through with the appeal."

"That's great news, but doesn't answer the question about Serena, does it? What'd you tell 'em?"

"She was fine. Funny, they knew about the car accident, though they didn't mention anything about Drury. The voice was disguised with some synthesizer, and they told me not to bother trying to trace the call, because it was a burner and they were going to destroy it as soon as our call was over."

"Covering all their bases. Whoever it is, they're smart."

Antonio agreed with his brother. Whoever the caller was seemed to know a lot about Big Jim and Serena. Which meant they were probably smack dab in the middle of the whole case.

"He texted me info on a bank in Dallas, where there's a safe deposit box containing all the information he or she has on Berkley."

"Do you think they're telling the truth?" Rafe's skepticism was apparent in his tone and his question. Antonio got it. Too much of this case had bordered on people lying, this might be one more person to add to the mix.

"My gut says yes."

"Do you think Williamson can get a warrant for the safe deposit box? Today's Sunday, which might be a problem."

"Here's the thing. The caller also overnighted a package. Said it contained notarized authorization for the safe deposit box and the key to the box. Get this, he's sending it to your office."

"You're kidding! Takes some big brass ones, I've gotta say."

"It's coming by private courier, so it'll probably get there pretty early. I plan on being at the sheriff's office bright and early. As soon as the package arrives, I'll head to Dallas and see what's in the safe deposit box."

"I'll go with you."

"Appreciate it, but, no. I need you to stay with Serena. Get her back to the Big House and keep her safe."

"Williamson can send FBI guys to—"

"Nope, this is too important to trust anybody else." Antonio paused, weighing his words carefully before he continued. "Bro, she's too important. I can't let anything happen to her. I've failed once, not keeping her safe. If anything happens to her, I…" He let his words trail off.

"I'll guard her with my life. Nobody will get to Serena. Nobody." He heard the resolve in his brother's voice, the promise he'd protect the woman Antonio loved. Because there was no denying it, no more hiding from the truth. He was in love with Serena Snowden, Sharon Berkley, whatever she wanted to call herself. He didn't care what her name was, he loved the woman he'd gotten to know over the past year. Somehow, some way, she'd snuck under his defenses and become as important to him as his next breath.

"Let's end this once and for all."

"What about Drury?"

Antonio scrubbed his hand over his face, and wished he was back home, instead of sitting in the traffic that hadn't moved in thirty minutes. He gave a self-deprecating laugh as he realized he'd thought about Shiloh Springs as home. Guess it helped make the decision which had been plaguing him for months. He wanted to come home for good.

"I've got somebody keeping an eye on him. He'll let me know if Drury does anything suspicious. A buddy from the Dallas office who volunteered to spend a couple of days watching the house and Drury. He's good."

"Then come home, bro."

"I am."

Coming home to stay.

CHAPTER NINETEEN

Antonio followed the guard back to the bank manager's office. The courier with the promised package had shown up at the sheriff's office at close to ten a.m., and only then after multiple phone calls to the company to get the courier there ASAP. He'd tossed around his weight with the FBI to light a fire under them, and had driven like a cat with its tail on fire straight through to Dallas, with the safe deposit box key and the authorization to access the box.

"Mr. Boudreau, I understand you have some paperwork I need to look at."

The bank manager stood in the open doorway leading to her office. A middle-aged woman in a business suit, she personified the stereotypical bank employee, right down to the sensible shoes and upswept hair style. Though she smiled, it didn't reach her eyes, and Antonio had the feeling she was going to be a real hard case.

"I have a letter authorizing me access to safe deposit box one six seven two nine. I also have the key for said box." He handed her the notarized document, and watched her do a cursory scan of its contents.

"I'll need to check our files. Please, come in." She walked around the big dark cherry-stained desk, its opulence and design spoke volumes about the wealth of the bank's customer base. The bank was housed in one of the large downtown buildings, right in the heart of Dallas, its chrome and glass and steel cold and impersonal, and probably owned the whole thing. Exactly the type of place somebody with oodles of money would think it safe.

Leaning against the doorjamb, he strove to appear non-chalant, though inside his emotions were a roiling pit of snakes. He tapped his cowboy hat against his thigh and took a deep breath, hoping against hope this information panned out and he hadn't been led on a wild goose chase by somebody after Serena. The bank manager typed away on the computer, verifying the information he'd provided. He really didn't want to waste any more time, but knew he needed to let the banker do her job, like he was doing his. Getting the goods on Berkley, keeping keep him behind bars, and keeping Serena safe was his number one priority, even if it meant playing nice with the bank.

"Mr. Boudreau, you are not listed as an authorized account user for this safe deposit box. I'm afraid—"

"Ma'am, the paperwork I presented you with is from the official account holder, authorizing my access to said safe deposit box. Access to the box is part of an ongoing FBI investigation. The appropriate notarized paperwork has been presented to a representative of the bank, namely you, and I have the key to said safety deposit box. Are you planning on impeding an FBI investigation and making me get a warrant? Because I can. I can also guarantee the feds will be all over your institution within a matter of hours, looking at every single piece of paperwork and every account you provide services for, resulting in some very unhappy customers."

She straightened in her leather-bound chair until Antonio swore he could use her spine as a yardstick, a pinched expression tightening her lips before it smoothed away to a conciliatory smirk.

Gotcha.

"That won't be necessary, Mr. Boudreau."

"Agent Boudreau."

"Agent Boudreau. Your paperwork appears to be in order. I'll personally accompany you and make sure there're no difficulties."

Antonio barely refrained from rolling his eyes at her rapid backpedaling. The woman knew when to do a strategic retreat, and how to keep her facility from being overrun with an onslaught of IRS and Treasury Department agents. Of course, he'd been bluffing, mostly. He could get a warrant, and he knew Williamson would throw his weight behind Antonio because the Berkley case was big news, and keeping the monster behind bars would have many in Washington lending all kinds of muscle to get the job done.

Antonio followed the manager and was led to a separate room, where rows upon rows of locked drawers lined the walls like little soldiers, their contents sealed and secured within the bank. His heartbeat sped up and he swallowed once, pushing down the surge of adrenaline flooding through his body. *This is it.* He felt it in his gut. Whatever was inside the safe deposit box would keep Serena safe. Let her come out from beneath the shadow of Big Jim Berkley once and for all.

In less than a minute, the drawer was opened and the box placed on the table in the center of the room. It looked too small to contain something monumental, innocuous and unassuming in its simplicity. The bank manager and the security guard who'd accompanied them turned and left, leaving him alone.

Anticipation warred with the need to take things slow, proceed with an eye toward caution. This could be a trap. He still didn't know who the mystery caller was or what his endgame might be. He hadn't recognized the name on the notarized authorization, pretty sure it an assumed name, but again it was something to work on later. He'd get the FBI on it, and figure out who the box really belonged to, but right here and right now, he had bigger fish to fry. He couldn't wait any longer. Knowledge was power, and he needed power to stop Big Jim Berkley permanently.

He wasn't sure what he expected when he flipped open the lid to the box. Certainly not the innocent-appearing envelope lying inside, sealed only with the metal clasp attached. His shoulders slumped as he reached inside, pulled out the sheath of papers and began flipping through each one.

With every page he scanned, his smile grew, because his mystery caller had been right. If this information was legit, it was enough—no, more than enough—to keep Big Jim locked away in solitary for the rest of his days.

Pulling out his cell phone, he snapped pics of each page. He wasn't taking any chances. He wanted backups of all the incriminating evidence against James Berkley. Backups of those backups. With the push of a button, he e-mailed them to SAC Williamson and to his brother, Rafe.

Shoving all the papers back into the envelope, he left the bank, feeling lighter than he had in days. For once, it looked like maybe the good guys were gonna win.

Big Jim shuffled down the hallway toward the visiting area. Hated the chains, what they represented. Restricting every movement. Inhibiting his freedom. They kept him shackled in the present, anchored to the here and now, and reminded him of his diminished power behind these prison walls. *But not for much longer.*

The orange jumpsuit would be the first thing to go, once the shackles got removed. He'd once again dress as befitting a man in his position, in the finest silks and designer suits, not scratchy cotton. Freedom was close enough he could feel its warm breath on his skin like a lover's caress. Patience had never been his strong suit, but he'd learned in his time behind bars to savor each small victory, because in the end, he'd come out a winner. Anything else was unacceptable.

The shove from the guard's hand in the middle of his back caused him to stumble, and he righted himself with a snarl. Instead of cowering in fear, which should have been the guard's first response, he laughed. Heat rose from the center of Big Jim's chest, flooding him with the desire to dig his hands into the guard's throat and tear the flesh from his bones. Yet he couldn't, not yet. Soon, it was only a matter of time, this guard and all the others like him would pay for the way they'd treated him. Once he was outside, walking free, he'd show them all what real fear felt like.

When they turned right at the hallway's intersection, he wondered what was going on, because they always turned left when taking him to see his lawyer. The rooms to the right had glass separating the prisoners from their visitors, whereas the rooms on the left were for the attorneys and their clients to have private, privileged conversations. A knot started forming in his gut. He didn't like this, not one bit.

When the guard opened the door, he looked down the row of chairs on his side of the glass dividing the prisoners from their guests. Most of the seats were occupied with inmates, spending their few precious moments of quality time with their loved ones. Further down the row, he spotted a familiar face, though it wasn't the one he'd been expecting.

ANTONIO

How he hated speaking through these phones to the person on the other side of the glass. It was hard to intimidate somebody when you couldn't get up close and personal, show them who was boss. Might not be necessary for this particular guest, though. She was somebody—special.

"Corinne, what are you doing here? I thought I was meeting with your husband."

"Change of plans, sweetie. Jonathan's dealing with his own problems right now. Did you know the FBI is breathing down his neck? Have you got any idea how hard it is to be married to somebody stupid?"

"What did he do?" Big Jim enunciated each word, spitting them out like bullets. Drury might be an excellent lawyer who knew every fine point of the law, but the man wasn't the sharpest wit outside the courtroom.

"The imbecile tried to kidnap Sharon. Can you believe it?"

He closed his eyes and counted to ten. "Tell me everything."

"Well, he told you I found her, right? I showed him the photo in the magazine." She smiled happily, practically bouncing in the chair. He made a moue of distaste, staring at her garish outfit, which was probably two sizes too small for her ever-expanding frame. Corinne had once been an attractive woman, and they'd had a brief fling, but she'd let herself go to seed. She'd always like having her ego stroked, which was one thing he could still do, no matter how distasteful.

"You did a wonderful job, Corinne. Jonathan sang your praises the last time he was here, and yes, he showed me the picture. Imagine, of all the people looking for Sharon, you were the only one who was able to find her."

"I know. She's been in some little town in Nowhere, Texas, all this time. I couldn't believe how different she looked with the darker hair, but I recognized her immediately. You can't fool me, I've got a great eye."

"Of course you do, sweetheart. Now, tell me about Jonathan and the FBI. You said he tried to kidnap her?"

Corinne preened beneath his attention, patting her stringy hair and batting her heavily mascaraed eyes his way. "He went to that town, Shiloh Springs. He said he found Sharon staying with a family there called the Boudreaus. He dug up all kinds of information on her, like the kind of car she drives, how she works for the real estate company, everything. Anyway, he knew she was staying with this Boudreau family on their ranch. Can you imagine Sharon living on a ranch?" She gave a shudder. "Jonathan said he parked along the road leading to the Boudreau ranch. Sat there for hours, waiting and watching. He'd almost given up when he spotted her car in the distance, coming toward him."

Big Jim could hear the rising excitement in Corinne's voice, her whole body practically vibrating with it. Leave it to Drury to pull some boneheaded stunt and have it backfire spectacularly, and get the FBI involved. He drummed his fingers on the countertop, his mind racing with possibilities. This was a bloody fiasco, but maybe he could make something good happen from it, he simply needed to think. Come up with the right angle to make things work in his favor.

"Go on, Corinne. What did Jonathan do next?"

"He sideswiped her car, forced her off the road. He swears he didn't hit it hard, he wasn't trying to hurt her. Anyway, she climbed out of her car and came over to check on him, thinking maybe he was hurt. She honest-to-goodness trotted over like a puppy. The plan was to snatch her up, stash her somewhere, then come and find out what you wanted done. Only his car got too damaged, and he was going to have to take hers."

"Wait, you're telling me he really did try and kidnap Sharon? Where'd he come up with such a seriously stupid move?" Corinne pulled back, leaning away from the glass, some of her excitement dimmed. He must've let too much of his anger seep into his voice. Now he had to do damage control, and stroke her ego, because he was going to need Corinne's cooperation to try and rectify the shambles her husband had made.

"He—he was only trying to help, Big Jim."

"I know, sweetheart. It's so hard, sitting behind these walls, unable to deal with things firsthand. And you're doing the right thing, bringing this to my attention. If the government thinks I had anything to do with trying to hurt Sharon, I'll never get my appeal heard."

A trembling smile blossomed on her lips, and he knew he had her back on the hook. He should have remembered he needed to use a gentle touch with Corinne, because as bold as she might project herself to others, underneath she was an insecure little girl thinking she could play with the big kids. The best plan of action, at least until he was sprung from this place, was to play along, let her believe in her own self-importance. She'd learn soon enough how very wrong she was about her place in his world—as would her husband.

"Tell me the rest. He obviously botched things, or the feds would be all over me, thinking I orchestrated the whole thing."

"Jonathan said Sharon took off running. There are woods and trees along that stretch of road, and she bolted after slamming his wrist in the car door. Poor thing is in so much pain."

He ain't seen nothing yet.

"He chased after her and grabbed her, but he said she hit her head on a tree branch, knocked herself out and wouldn't wake up. Then he heard some men in the woods, and he got spooked. He took off and one of them chased him all the way to the street. He was smart though, and stole Sharon's car to get away."

"How is that smart, Corinne? The cops are going to be looking it and for Jonathan."

She emphatically shook her head, leaning close to the glass and spoke in an almost whisper into the phone. "He ditched the car in a shopping center. And he swears the guy chasing him didn't get close enough for a good look at his face. Cousin Phil drove down and picked him up and drove him back home."

"What about Sharon?"

Corinne bit her lip, and didn't meet his gaze. "We don't know what happened to her. I—I called a couple of hospitals, but there's no record of Sharon Berkley or Serena Snowden, the name she uses in Texas."

His thoughts were a blur, racing one after the next. If she'd died, he'd have heard from one of his contacts. Which meant she was still alive, at least for the moment. He needed her alive a little while longer. Long enough to gain access to the money in the Cayman Islands' account. He needed that money. The DOJ had frozen every one of his assets, hundreds of millions of dollars, and without the infusion of funds from the offshore bank, all his contacts, his hackers, would dry up and evaporate, because nobody did anything out of the goodness of their hearts. People weren't kind and generous and giving souls. They were black-hearted, greedy, avaricious, money-hungry sharks who'd sell you out to the next highest bidder who came along.

"Corinne, you said the FBI came to see you. What exactly did they want?"

"They wanted to shake Jonathan's alibi, wanted me to

tell them he hadn't been home when the accident happened. The FBI agent was hot, and he flirted outrageously with me, but I didn't tell him anything."

"Good." He stood, and the guard took a step toward him. "Tell Jonathan I want to see him. We have a few things to discuss about my upcoming appeal." He contemplated her carefully, knowing as much as he wanted to toss her to the wolves, he'd need her when he got out, at least in the beginning. After—well, who knew what might happen.

Dropping the phone into its cradle, he shuffled out the door and headed back to his cell, the guard following close behind. He could last a little longer. Because he was going to come out on top this time, and then they'd pay. They'd all pay.

CHAPTER TWENTY

Serena settled into the rocking chair in the living room with a sigh of contentment. Doc Stevens released her from the clinic, and Douglas showed up within minutes of the paperwork being signed, ready to deliver her back to the ranch. The FBI agent Williamson had assigned to guard her stood by, watching every movement of the clinic's staff, and she'd heard him ask Douglas for identification before he'd been allowed into her room. The agent followed them to the ranch, and was now ensconced in the kitchen with a cup of coffee and some baked goods. Ms. Patti never let anybody in her house go hungry.

It felt good to be back at the ranch. The minute they'd driven through the large gate leading to the Boudreau property, she'd felt her world shift on its axis and everything felt right again. Driving up the long stretch of road, past the pastures filled with animals a sense of peace swept through her, and her soul felt like she was coming home.

She'd spotted Dane headed out of the barn as the car pulled up in front of the Big House. He'd smiled and waved before climbing onto his saddled horse. Liam followed close behind, and he dipped his head before riding out. Talking to Ms. Patti in the past, she knew the ranch raised cattle, and leased land to the government for horses. They also hired several ranch hands year-round, keeping the whole operation running.

Serena felt guilty about rushing off and leaving Ridge behind, and planned on apologizing profusely when she saw him again. She glanced up when she heard a noise, and smiled as Ms. Patti walked in, carrying a loaded tray, placing it on the footrest in front of her chair. A pitcher of tea and ice-filled glasses and a plate of cookies. Looking closely, she shook her head and laughed softly, because the cookies were oatmeal raisin. Her favorite. She honestly didn't know how Ms. Patti managed to do everything she did: run a business, handle a whole crew of ranch hands, deal with a daughter in college, and even though all her sons were grown didn't mean she didn't still run them with an iron fist couched in a velvet glove. All that, in addition to being the town's matriarch. She knew everything going on in Shiloh Springs—everything. Nothing happened in her town she didn't know about as soon as it happened. There were whispers a lot of the town folk thought she was psychic.

"With everything going on, I forgot to ask. Did somebody help out Mr. Olson?"

Ms. Patti chuckled and slid onto the love seat across from Serena's rocker. "Believe it or not, in all the confusion, Douglas was the one who remembered poor Mr. Olson. He's fine, by the way. He waited around for you, and when you didn't show, he went alone and viewed the property. After all his hemming and hawing for years, he decided he didn't want to buy the place after all."

"You're kidding? He's been after that place ever since I moved to Shiloh Springs."

"Sometimes we build things up in our minds, make them bigger and better than they actually are." Ms. Patti picked up a glass and poured the tea and handed it to Serena, then fixed one for herself. "Have you heard from my son?"

"Not yet. He told me he got a tip and headed to Dallas. I hope he gets back soon."

The sound of the front door opening had Serena glancing toward the opening, surprised when Rafe walked in. "Afternoon, ladies."

"Son. What brings you by?"

"I talked with Antonio. He's on his way. Should be home soon, once he gets through all the Dallas construction."

Serena started to stand, but sank back into her chair at Rafe's glare. "He's okay? Did he find anything?"

Rafe moved to sit on the loveseat beside Ms. Patti, giving her a quick kiss on the cheek, and snatched a cookie off the plate. "He's going to want to tell you all the details in person, but let's say it wasn't a wasted trip."

"Boy, you better tell me more if you ever expect me to cook for you again." Ms. Patti folded her arms across her chest, her eyes firmly on Rafe.

"Momma, you know I can't talk about an ongoing investigation." He turned his head and winked at Serena. "But since it's not actually my investigation, I'll tell you what I can. Antonio got an anonymous tip yesterday. Somebody claimed to have enough incriminating evidence to keep Big Jim Berkley behind bars and derail any efforts he might entertain for an appeal."

"A tip? Did it seem legit?" Serena cradled her wrapped wrist against her chest and scooted forward, studying Rafe intently. When he was in sheriff mode, he was nearly impossible to read, and right now, his face was an inscrutable mask, except for the hint of humor in his eyes, which he didn't attempt to hide.

"I'm not at liberty to divulge what Antonio may or may not have found," he said, holding up both hands, palms out, "but I'll go out on a limb and say the government is going to be happy."

"Does it mean Serena's safe? That's all I care about."

Rafe wrapped his arm around his mother's shoulder. "Serena's never going to have to worry about Big Jim or any of his lunatic fringe ever again."

"Son, that's the best news! I'm going to make you the biggest pan of banana pudding you've ever seen. And you don't have to share."

Rafe grinned and rubbed his hands together. "I love being the bearer of good news. I get all the rewards and none of the flack."

The screech of tires outside brought everybody on their feet, racing for the door. Serena heard the thud of boots against the wooden porch before she made it to the front door. It swung inward, and Antonio stood in the doorway, his eyes meeting hers, his lips curved upward in a slow grin.

"Sweetheart, we've got him!" Rushing forward, he pulled her into his arms, lifted her off the ground and spun her around. "There's enough evidence to put him away and keep the feds chasing going after his followers for years to come. It's all over but the shouting."

"I can't believe it! It's really over?"

"I e-mailed copies of everything to Williamson in Austin. Sent another sent to Rafe. I have the originals under lock and key in my own safe deposit box in Dallas, which I'll turn over to Williamson in the morning. I didn't want to drive back with them, in case somebody tried to pull something. But it's over. There's no way Big Jim escapes wearing an orange jumpsuit for the rest of his natural life."

Serena sagged in his arms, relief swamping her. Her nightmare was ending. She was finally free.

Antonio led her back into the living room and helped her into the rocking chair. He moved the tray to the floor and sat on the footrest in front of her. Taking her free hand in his, he ignored his mother and brother, who stood in the opening to the living room, his focus solely on her.

"You'll need to stay here for a while longer, until all the

paperwork has been disseminated and verified. Williamson assured me they're going after Drury too. They found his fingerprints all over the wrecked rental car, and they've got footage from the security cameras at the car rental place. He didn't do the actual rental, his wife did, under the name Sharon Berkley."

Serena started at Antonio's words. "Corinne used my name? Why on earth would she try and pretend to be me? It would raise all kinds of red flags with the people looking for me."

"A question for Williamson to ask her, but she had identification with your name and your information, so it wasn't a random act. Makes me think the Drury's had their own agenda."

"Maybe it has something to do with what Jonathan said, about me being his ticket to freedom, though I'd have to think about it some more. I don't care, as long as my uncle stays behind bars, and can't hurt anybody ever again, that's what matters."

"Even with the best attorneys money can buy, he's not getting out of prison. Nobody was killed in the bombings, which was a miracle in itself, but—he has killed. I'm sorry, Serena, but the evidence in the safe deposit box outlines multiple people who were murdered on his orders."

Serena stared at him, the words sinking in, a hollow acknowledgement of what she'd always suspected. Her uncle was a cold, calculating monster with no regard for human life or the wants and needs of others. An awful thought pushed its way to the front of her mind, and she couldn't shake it, didn't want to voice the question. But could she really live with herself if she didn't?

"The people he had killed, was one of them my mother?"

Antonio shook his head. "I looked, but didn't see anything about her. I remembered you saying she went missing when you were little. There isn't anything to indicate what happened to her."

Serena closed her eyes, trying to picture her mother's face, but it had been too many years since her mother had disappeared from her life. Her father insisted she'd run off with somebody else, but Serena had never believed it, not for a minute. It seemed a shame her mother wasn't around to see Big Jim get what was coming to him.

When she looked up, Rafe and Ms. Patti had disappeared, leaving her and Antonio alone in the living room.

"It still hasn't sunk in, that it's all over. No more hiding. No more running away, afraid all the time. It's kinda surreal, but in the best way."

"Does that mean you'll stay here?"

"Wow, I've never really thought far ahead, if I'm being honest. Never let my guard down, because it was temporary and I knew I'd have to leave. Living in Shiloh Springs, it's been the longest I've stayed in one place since the trial ended. Even when I bought the townhouse, I knew in the back of my mind I'd have to leave it behind one day. Now, I don't know what I'm going to do."

"Stay."

His words, the way he said them, sent a shiver down her spine. Not in fear. But hope.

"You want me to stay?"

"More than anything. I've been thinking about it for a while, and I'm moving back to Shiloh Springs. I've never been happy in Dallas, and I miss it here. I talked with SAC Williamson, and I'm going to transfer to the Austin office. Most of the time, I'll be commuting a few times a week, and part of the time, I'll work from here. We'll work out the finer points, but I'm coming home."

"That's wonderful, Antonio. Your family will be happy to have you here. I know Ms. Patti has missed you."

He stood and pulled her to her feet, and wrapped an arm around her waist, pulling her closer. Leaning in, he whispered, "A big part of my coming home is you, Serena. There's been something between us from the day we met. I fought it because long distance relationships rarely work out, and I was too focused on advancing up the ranks in the FBI. But every time I came home, every time I saw you, those feelings grew and intensified. This last time, when I found out who you really are, and the danger you were in, all I could think about was making sure you were safe, because the thought of living in a world where you weren't a part of my life—I couldn't bear it."

"I thought I was the only one. Every time I saw you, it

was like I don't know how to describe it, like the missing part of my soul was found and I was finally whole."

"Exactly. Say you'll stay, give us a chance." He cupped her face gently between his hands, and Serena felt the intensity of his stare down to her toes. "I'm head over heels in love with you, Serena Snowden."

Finally, she could say the words, the ones she'd know to be true for so long. "I love you too, Antonio Boudreau. I think I fell in love with you the day we met, and I can't imagine what my life would be like without you. I've dreaded waking up each day, thinking about leaving you, this town, and everything I've come to love. I can't believe it's finally over, and my every dream is coming true."

"For goodness sake, would you kiss her already, before Momma has a heart attack out here in the hallway!" Rafe's laughter echoed through the living room along with Ms. Patti's huff of outrage.

"My pleasure."

When his lips touched hers, Serena knew everything was going to be alright, and surrendered herself to his kiss, and for the first time looked to the future with hope.

CHAPTER TWENTY-ONE

Serena sat at the long conference table set up for the meeting. Antonio clasped her hand tight, giving her a modicum of composure. She both dreaded the upcoming meeting and wanted to be here, because this would be the last time she had to see her uncle face-to-face. His cadre of attorneys lined one side of the table, in their expensive suits, briefcases filled with what she assumed were reams of papers to try and offset the insurmountable evidence against him.

Antonio and Williamson had shown her the mountain of evidence provided by the mysterious informant, who'd cooperated with the Department of Justice once the file had been hand delivered to their office. Serena had no clue who this person was, only they were a 'credible' witness from deep within her uncle's fanatical followers. She hoped she'd get the chance to meet with them, thank them for doing the right thing, especially since it meant she didn't have to go through another excruciating trial. Once had been more than enough. When added to the information she'd provided Williamson on the thumb drive, she prayed this would be the last time she ever faced her uncle again.

There were several other people, men and women, seated at the table. Antonio whispered they were DOJ, and attorney generals for several of the states where bombings had taken place.

"Are you sure you want to be here, Serena? You don't have to face him, you know. I can get you out of here. We'll go someplace, just the two of us, and forget all about Big Jim or anything else except us."

She gave him a shaky smile. "I need to be here. It's important. He needs to see he didn't win. He didn't break me, no matter how hard he tried. His personal empire is crumbling around him, and there's no way out. He's a broken man, he just doesn't know it yet."

"Jonathan Drury and his wife are going to spend time behind bars. Drury's copping a plea to attempted kidnapping, use of a deadly weapon—both vehicular and a gun—along with several other assorted charges. He'll spend a lot of years behind bars. Corinne's pleading to identity theft, yours, and a few other charges. Since it's her first offense, she'll probably get a light sentence, but it's better than nothing."

She knew the district attorney had arrested Jonathan and had him extradited to Texas, since both he and Corinne were in Oklahoma City. Corinne would face charges only in Oklahoma. It still didn't make sense why Drury had come after her. Maybe she'd never know.

The door swung open, and several guards stepped through, followed by Big Jim Berkley. He towered over most of the people there, but Serena wasn't intimidated by him. Not anymore. No, she wasn't giving him the power to make her life a living nightmare, not since she'd seen everything he'd done. She'd always thought him a monster—now there was concrete proof she was right.

He smirked when he spotted her across the room, and held up one hand as far as the attached chain allowed. "Hello, Sharon. It's been a long time."

"Not long enough," she shot back.

"Everyone sit down, and we'll get started. Present are James Berkley and his legal representation, Derrick Williamson and Antonio Boudreau from the FBI, and Sharon Berkley, aka Serena Snowden, William Hanover and Clarence Lark from the Department of Justice. SAC Williamson, please begin."

"Thank you, sir. The FBI has provided evidence obtained from a confidential informant conclusively proving James Berkley, alias Big Jim Berkley, was instrumental in the deaths of six people—"

"Objection." One of Big Jim's attorneys started to stand, and Williamson glared at him.

"Sit down. This is an informal hearing to provide you with all the new information we've received. If you'll keep your mouth shut, we'll get through this quicker, and you can meet with your client and tell him how far up the creek he is, without any chance of getting off this wild ride, got it? Good."

Serena bit back her laughter at the sight of her uncle's face. Beet red, he was shocked and outraged, sputtering at Williamson's verbal barrage. If she wasn't madly in love with Antonio, she'd so go out with Williamson. She gave Antonio's hand a squeeze to let him know she was handling things alright.

"Enclosed in your packets are copies of the information provided by our informants. They give names, dates, meeting places, as well as photographic evidence confirming each hit. There are transcribed reports of recordings of Mr. Berkley and his known associates discussing said assassinations, as well as Mr. Berkley ordering them. There are outlined account records of money laundering. In addition, there are copies of blueprints and photographs, along with employee schedules, for the buildings that were bombed."

One of her uncle's lawyers stood and glared at Williamson. "We have a problem with the FBI and the DOJ using a confidential informant. How do we know this information is reliable? Our client has the right to face his accuser. I don't see anyone here who could provide you with this kind of information, the veracity of which has yet to be determined. I suggest this information is tainted, fruit from the poisoned tree, and completely unsubstantiated without corroboration."

One of the representatives from the Department of Justice reached into his pocket and pulled out a cell phone. "Send her in."

A few moments later, the door opened and a tall, elegantly dressed woman strode through. When Berkley spotted her, a string of curses spewed forth, but Serena ignored him and everything else around her, her vision shrinking like a tunnel, focused solely on the woman standing silhouetted in the open doorway.

"Mom?"

She felt more than saw Antonio's stiffening in shock, but couldn't take her eyes off the woman, as chaos erupted in the room. Everyone was talking at once, each trying to be heard over the other in a cacophony of louder and louder objections, but Serena didn't care. Her mother gave her a soft smile, her blue eyes shining with love.

"I said quiet down!" The DOJ representative slammed a book onto the table with a loud bang. Big Jim fought against the guards, trying to keep him in his chair, curses still spewing from his lips.

"Gentlemen, as you can see, our confidential informant is Christine Berkley, James Berkley's stepsister. We will be scheduling a time and place for a deposition at our earliest convenience. I suggest you confer with your client, and make sure he understands the gravity of the charges leveled against him, as well as the postponement of his appeal." He glared at the attorneys all huddled around Big Jim. "You'll also find additional information pertaining to a new set of charges being filed against Mr. Berkley, including bribery of a federal judge."

"What documentation do you have to make sure allegations against our client?"

A DVD was tossed onto the table. "The Department of Justice, along with the FBI, have been provided with video footage of James Berkley meeting with federal judge Hiram Coleman, and exchanging money to ensure Judge Coleman tampered with the court schedule and presided over Mr. Berkley's case and sentencing. The judge's wife was also present at said meeting, and she'll be facing charges of abuse of her position as a state congresswoman. Despite Mr. Berkley's attempts to monetarily influence the judicial system, justice prevailed. Take a very good look at the video footage I just provided you with, gentlemen, because it is clear and explicit and damning to your client."

"That's impossible!" Big Jim's face drained of all color, and he appeared to shrivel before Serena's eyes.

"It's entirely possible, Uncle. I took the video. I witnessed the meeting, and I'll be happy to testify against you and your corrupt friends." Serena's confidence grew with each word. She was finally free from the terror her uncle inspired for far too long, fear that had kept her frozen. Now he was nothing more than a pathetic petty tyrant whose kingdom had crumbled into ashes at his feet.

The DOJ representative glared at Big Jim's attorneys, and made a shooing motion. "We're done here."

"This isn't over!" Big Jim shouted as the guards dragged him to his feet. "I'll kill you all! Especially you, you duplicitous traitor!" He lunged for Christine, and the guards yanked him back and shuffled him out the door. Everyone else followed suit, leaving Serena and Antonio alone with her mother.

"I don't understand. How can you be here?"

Her mother sat in the chair beside Serena and took her hand, clasping it between hers. "Oh, my sweet baby, there's so much to tell you. I didn't want to leave you, but I didn't have a choice. Your uncle has always been power mad, and he'd do anything to get more. When I discovered what he planned, he—he tried to have me killed."

"Mom! Did you go to the police?"

Christine nodded. "Of course, but I didn't know he had the chief of police in his back pocket. My brother had dirt on half the influential people in town, and the other half were scared to death of him. The chief took my statement, and the next thing I knew, I was grabbed on my way out of the grocery store. I was taken to an old barn and tied up for days. I knew my brother would come put a bullet in my head when he was ready. I managed to get away, and I ran. When I tried to contact Abner, your father told me I was dead to him. He must have divorced me somehow, because you know he remarried. I changed my name, did odd jobs here and there, and tried to live a normal life. None of that's important. I met a wonderful man a few years after I ran." Serena wanted to ask the question burning inside, but didn't dare. The answer might hurt too much.

"Why didn't you take Sharon with you?" Trust Antonio to know exactly what she'd been thinking.

"I wanted to. Every single day I missed you. A couple of times I even drove by the house, trying to catch a glimpse of you. I tried to come up with a plan where I could take you with me, but I knew it wouldn't be safe. You didn't deserve to live a life on the run, where I might not be able to keep you from harm. Jim had guards all around the place, watching, waiting for me to make a mistake. He knew I'd try to come back for you. If there had been any way, if I didn't think Jim wouldn't hunt for us every single day, I'd have risked everything. But I know your father loved you. Leaving you behind was the hardest thing I've ever done, and I've regretted it every day. I did it to keep you safe. I never expected your father to drag you into Jim's web of lies."

"How did you end up getting dirt on my uncle?"

Christine smiled and brushed her hair over her shoulder. The soft blonde color, so similar to Serena's natural color, made it obvious they were related, and Serena almost reached out to touch it, see if it was as soft as she remembered from her childhood.

"I met someone. A wonderful man who helped me see the good in people again. I was jaded, distrustful, and believed most people were exactly like your uncle. Out for money and power, and didn't care about anybody or anything except themselves. It took me a long time to open myself, to trust him. Isaac worked for the government, an aide for a senator. Once he heard my story, he convinced me to talk to the senator. She asked if I'd be willing to help take down my brother. I had to say yes. What else could I do? I knew Jim better than anybody else, knew what he was capable of. It was only a matter of time before he killed people. It was inevitable."

Serena nodded. She agreed with her mother's assessment, because she'd felt the same. If only she'd known her mother was out there, alive and gathering evidence. It looked like they were cut from the same cloth, as the saying goes, because they'd had the same goal.

"The senator had me contact somebody from the old days. It was a huge risk, because if word got back to Jim, things might have gone completely differently. I slowly ingratiated myself within the lower ranks. Changed my looks. I was heavier, I wore a wig and glasses. Nobody recognized me, and I stayed quiet and meek, making my way unobtrusively around until I became a fixture in the background there, so nobody paid attention to me. Before long, they started talking freely whenever I was around. Even my brother didn't recognize me, because I looked so different from the polished, sophisticated woman I'd been before he tried to have me killed."

"I've always known he was evil, but I thought he was loyal to family." Serena shrugged but had a hard time containing her shock.

"I began sneaking my cell phone into meetings, and

recording everything. Most days the information was useless, but when Jim gets angry, he tends to get mouthy, too. He'd make mistakes, forget I was there. Remember, everybody around him was loyal to a fault. Nobody crossed Jim. I recorded things that would make you blush. I took photos of things when nobody was looking. Jim was careful, always so careful. But others weren't. Every few days, I turned the information over to the senator, but I kept my own file." Christine's eyes filled with tears. "I can't tell you how thrilled I was when he was arrested. Until I found out you'd be testifying against him."

"I had to. I was the only one who had enough information to take him down. No one had a clue you were doing the same thing I was, collecting evidence. I don't remember ever seeing you."

"That's one of the things which took so long. I couldn't go back to Oklahoma. Everybody would recognize me, even with the disguise. I hung out at the Louisiana compound." She grinned. "He hated anybody calling his precious center a compound. Wouldn't let anybody say it. Made it sound too much like a cult, with him as the leader. Idiot didn't recognize it for what it was, a stinking cult." Her smile dimmed as she continued. "I didn't have enough evidence at the time to come forward. It wouldn't have mattered anyway. The senator I gave the information to ended up stockpiling all the data, and when she had enough, took it to Jim. Tried to blackmail him. You can guess how well that went."

Antonio's hand rested on Serena's shoulder. "Are you talking about Senator Wellsley? The one who died in a plane crash?"

Christine nodded again. "I was terrified. Jim knew there was a traitor in his organization, and I had no choice but to leave. Then the trial happened and your life turned upside down. Isaac, bless his heart, knew a couple of people who worked for the FBI, so I knew when you went into witness protection. I've kept my eye on you as best I could from a distance, baby."

"How'd you know to contact me?" Antonio threw the question out, and Christine leaned back in her chair, smoothing a hand along her tailored skirt. She was dressed like a modern professional woman, with a tailored suit, narrow pencil skirt and black pumps. She might have walked straight out of any office and nobody would have thought about it twice.

"My...friend, Isaac. Did I mentioned he has a few friends in the FBI? He said there was an increased push on to find Sharon, especially since Jim was getting his case appealed. There seemed to be a lot of activity in the Austin office, searching for her. I have a few contacts of my own, friends who work in the intelligence community, in a not-so-visible fashion. So we kept our attention on Austin. Heard about you being assigned the case."

"Seems like a lot of coincidences, so again, why me?"

"You piqued my interest when you visited Jonathan Drury's house. The little piss-ant might be a good lawyer,

212

but he's not the smartest cookie in the jar. When you started sniffing around him, I knew something happened. I—took a gamble when I called you. My sources said you were reliable. He did mention you have quite a colorful family. I think the Boudreaus impressed him."

"You trusted me with the evidence. Why?"

"Because when I asked, you were honest with me. Reluctant, but honest when I asked about my daughter. I needed somebody I could trust. My gut told me you'd do the right thing."

Serena leaned forward, inhaling the subtle scent of her mother's perfume. It was the same one she'd worn when Serena was little, and it evoked memories of happier times when she was young. "What happens now? Where will you go?"

"I'll have to stick around, be available to the feds for a while. After? I don't know. I hope you'll want to see me." Her words trailed off, more a question than a statement.

"Of course I want to see you. You're my mom." Serena put her arms around her mother, hugged her, and sighed when her mother wrapped her arms around Serena, squeezing her back. "You can come to Shiloh Springs. It's a lovely town, and I know there are some people who'll want to meet you."

"More Boudreaus?" her mother quipped.

Serena laughed before replying. "Oh, yeah, more Boudreaus."

CHAPTER TWENTY-TWO
EPILOGUE

B rody leaned against the wooden pole of the pergola, and watched the assembled group around him. The weather was beautiful, the sun shining down on the happy couple. The family had invited practically the whole town to celebrate Rafe and Tessa's engagement. He wasn't surprised Rafe popped the question. His brother had been head-over-heels over the redheaded schoolteacher from the moment she'd moved to Shiloh Springs. Theirs had been more or less a whirlwind courtship, fraught with danger and intrigue, but true love prevailed in the end. His big brother was getting the happily ever after he deserved.

His mind wandered back to his job, where it seemed to be most of the time anymore. The fire department was down a couple of men, one with a broken right leg and right arm, and another from a concussion. He needed every able-bodied man, because somebody was intentionally starting fires around Shiloh Springs. So far, things had been contained, though after the last one, he suspected arson. No one had been injured in the first blaze, though a few of the buildings had major property damage. If it continued, he'd have to call in an arson investigator from either Austin or Dallas, because so far he hadn't been able to piece together the few clues he had to point to a suspect. But he wasn't giving up. He knew he needed to move fast, get a handle on things before somebody ended up hurt—or worse—in the blazes being set.

He shook himself free from thoughts of work and straightened, watching Rafe and Tessa, Rafe's arm around Tessa's waist. Now wasn't the time to dwell on work. This was a party, festivities for the happy couple, with dancing, food and family. The food part was over, and now the party was ramping up. A local band played country music in the background. A few couples filled the center of the wooden deck, swaying to the music. Rafe and Tessa, Dad and Momma, even the Fergusons were out on the dance floor, though they barely moved, simply holding each other in their arms. Off to the side, he watched Antonio tug Serena into his arms, her face alight with laughter.

He couldn't remember the last time he'd seen his brother so happy. He'd taken the long road to get there, and it had been a bumpy trip, but like Rafe and Tessa, they'd made it out to the other side. Antonio was moving back home, which made his dad and momma happier than he'd seen them in a long time.

"Rafe and Tessa, they're so happy, they practically glow."

Brody slid his arm around his little sister's shoulders. Nica had arrived that afternoon, making it home from college. She'd claimed she couldn't believe her brother was getting engaged, and wanted to see for herself before she'd believe it.

"They are happy. Antonio got word this morning Big Jim Berkley's appeal won't happen, and he's pleading guilty to a laundry list of additional charges, including the murder of Senator Wellsley. Serena is finally safe."

Nica wrapped her arm around his waist and leaned her head against his shoulder. "I missed out on everything. Who knew Serena wasn't even Serena? I'm stuck at school while everybody else gets to have all the fun."

"Listen, shrimp, I wouldn't call being in witness protection and then having to be on the run, being hunted by your own family, having fun."

"Well, not that part, obviously. I meant the falling in love part. Momma said watching Antonio and Serena dance around each other for the last year has been like watching a soap opera. Add in the feds, car crashes, death threats, a long-lost mother reappearing, and it sounds more like a movie of the week, but whatever."

"It all worked out in the end. I wouldn't be surprised if Antonio doesn't pop the question soon. Nothing would make Momma happier. She'd get another new daughter-in-law and keep her working at Boudreau Realty."

"Wow, you're such a romantic, Brody. *Not.* I'm going to head over and grab a piece of cake. Want anything?"

He leaned over and pressed a kiss on the top of her head.

"Nope. I'm good."

Staring up at him, she whispered, "Yes, you are. Don't ever forget it. Love ya!"

He watched her practically skip over to the dessert table, where a huge engagement cake provided by Jill Monroe, Tessa's best friend, sat in the middle. Even he had to admit it was a work of art in cake form. Jill had some serious chops when it came to baking, and it tasted even better than it looked.

A trill of laughter drew his gaze, and his lips quirked up when he spotted Jamie, Beth's little girl. Beth and Jamie came back for Tessa's engagement party, having gone home to North Carolina not long ago. The lower half of Jamie's face was covered with frosting, and Beth chuckled while using a napkin to clean it off her wiggling daughter. Beth's blonde hair was pulled up, leaving her cheekbones and neckline exposed, and she looked beautiful in a soft lavender one-shoulder dress. She was beautiful. An earth goddess with a heart-stopping smile.

Too bad she was off limits.

Thank you for reading Antonio, Book #2 in the Texas Boudreau Brotherhood series. I hope you enjoyed Antonio and Serena's story. Want to find out more about *Brody Boudreau and the excitement and adventure he's about to plunge headfirst into*? Keep reading for an excerpt from his book, *Brody, Book #3 in the Texas Boudreau Brotherhood. Available at all major e-book and print vendors.*

Brody (Texas Boudreau Brotherhood series)
© Kathy Ivan

After tossing and turning for a couple of hours, any thoughts of actual sleep disappeared. Brody headed to the kitchen, and reached for the coffee pot, pouring a cup. Strong and black, just the way he liked it. Standing in the open back doorway, he stared out at the sweeping panorama of the Boudreau ranch. He loved the old place, felt the connection deep in his soul, and if circumstances were different, he'd probably choose to live here permanently. Work with the horses and the cattle and been happy. But he was compelled, some might even call it obsessed, to work with fire. Saving people, saving buildings, it was a calling he couldn't ignore.

Finishing his coffee, he spotted his father walking toward the barn, his stride purposeful, his ever-present cowboy hat pulled low over his brow. The sight evoked a memory from early days, when he'd first come to live at the Big House. While Douglas owned and ran a large and extremely successful construction company, he was as much a part of the working ranch as the dirt beneath his boots. He'd lost count of the times he'd seen the man working alongside the ranch hands, setting posts and mending fences, doing his fair share to keep their homestead running.

Douglas Boudreau held a special place in Brody's heart, had from the day he'd met him. Bigger than life, tall and strong, to a small eight-year-old boy the mountain of a man engendered an imposing and intimidating sight, yet he'd learned quickly Douglas Boudreau was one of the gentlest men Brody ever met. With a heart as big as Texas, Douglas and Ms. Patti welcomed him into their home and into their hearts, with an ease he found remarkable to this day. He couldn't put into words the special place in his heart these two remarkable people held, helping him bridge the painful gap of heartbreak and loss at a tender age. Some days he could feel Ms. Patti's loving arms wrapped around him while he'd mourned, sharing his grief, his young mind unable to accept the devastating loss and changes, the yawning despair threatening to swallow him whole.

Shaking his head, he rinsed his cup, put it in the dishwasher, and headed out to the barn. Maybe a little strenuous exercise might help clear his head, make sense of the jumbled thoughts rolling around inside his brain.

While he'd tried in vain to sleep, all he'd thought about, fantasized about, was Beth Stewart. Beautiful, headstrong, and independent, she'd moved halfway across the country to make a clean break with painful memories and a messy divorce. She was making a new life for her and her daughter in a new town under strained and stressful circumstances. Though she'd been welcomed as part of the Boudreau family, he didn't feel anything close to familial about the feisty woman who kept him fantasizing about a future which could never be.

When Brody walked into the barn, Douglas sat atop a wooden stool hold a bridle, studying it with the same intensity he did everything else. The worn leather looked tiny within his father's big, work-roughened hands. His dad looked up when Brody walked in, his face a study of lines and angles, tanned from working outdoors his entire life. Years in the military as an Army Ranger trained and disciplined him into a strong man, one with a compassionate heart and an easy smile. Hands toughened and scarred from construction work, as well as daily life on the ranch, their touch could yield a gentleness belied by his size, or a swat to a backside when deserved.

"Morning, son. Heard you had a tough night."

"That it was, Dad. Blaze at the Summers' Place. A bad

one. Thankfully, we caught it in time before it spread too far."

"It's a shame, place lying abandoned like that. It's a good piece of property. Any idea what caused it?"

Brody hesitated, not wanting to make any unfounded assumptions, but his father knew the lay of the land when it came to things happening in and around Shiloh Springs. He'd spent most of his adult life here after leaving the military, and was well respected by everyone in their small community. He also had a good head on his shoulders when it came to people. Soft spoken and not given to saying much, when he did offer his opinion, people listened. Douglas sometimes reminded him of a throwback to a different time, when a man's word meant something. His father was a fair man, one who he trusted implicitly, and knew whatever he told Douglas would be kept between them.

"I don't have any proof yet, but I think the fire was deliberately set."

LINKS TO BUY:

www.kathyivan.com/books.html

NEWSLETTER SIGN UP

Don't want to miss out on any new books, contests, and free stuff? Sign up to get my newsletter. I promise not to spam you, and only send out notifications/e-mails whenever there's a new release or contest/giveaway. Follow the link and join today!

http://eepurl.com/baqdRX

REVIEWS ARE IMPORTANT!

People are always asking how they can help spread the word about my books. One of the best ways to do that is by word of mouth. Tell your friends about the books and recommend them. Share them on Goodreads. If you find a book or series or author you love – talk about it. Everybody loves to find out about new books and new-to-them authors, especially if somebody they know has read the book and loved it.

The next best thing is to write a review. Writing a review for a book does not have to be long or detailed. It can be as simple as saying "I loved the book."

I hope you enjoyed reading Brody, Texas Boudreau Brotherhood.

If you liked the story, I hope you'll consider leaving a review for the book at the vendor where you purchased it and at Goodreads. Reviews are the best way to spread the word to others looking for good books. It truly helps.

BOOKS BY KATHY IVAN

www.kathyivan.com/books.html

TEXAS BOUDREAU BROTHERHOOD
Rafe

Antonio

Brody

NEW ORLEANS CONNECTION SERIES
Desperate Choices

Connor's Gamble

Relentless Pursuit

Ultimate Betrayal

Keeping Secrets

Sex, Lies and Apple Pies

Deadly Justice

Wicked Obsession

Hidden Agenda

Spies Like Us

Fatal Intentions

New Orleans Connection Series Box Set: Books 1-3

New Orleans Connection Series Box Set: Books 4-7

CAJUN CONNECTION SERIES
Saving Sarah

Saving Savannah

Saving Stephanie

Guarding Gabi

LOVIN' LAS VEGAS SERIES
It Happened In Vegas

Crazy Vegas Love

Marriage, Vegas Style

A Virgin In Vegas

Vegas, Baby!

Yours For The Holidays

Match Made In Vegas

One Night In Vegas

Last Chance In Vegas

Lovin' Las Vegas (box set books 1-3)

OTHER BOOKS BY KATHY IVAN
Second Chances (Destiny's Desire Book #1)

Losing Cassie (Destiny's Desire Book #2)

ABOUT THE AUTHOR

USA TODAY Bestselling author Kathy Ivan spent most of her life with her nose between the pages of a book. It didn't matter if the book was a paranormal romance, romantic suspense, action and adventure thrillers, sweet & spicy, or a sexy novella. Kathy turned her obsession with reading into the next logical step, writing.

Her books transport you to the sultry splendor of the French Quarter in New Orleans in her award-winning romantic suspense, or to Las Vegas in her contemporary romantic comedies. Kathy's new romantic suspense series features, Texas Boudreau Brotherhood, features alpha heroes in small town Texas. Gotta love those cowboys!

Kathy tells stories people can't get enough of; reuniting old loves, betrayal of trust, finding kidnapped children, psychics and sometimes even a ghost or two. But one thing they all have in common – love and a happily ever after).

More about Kathy and her books can be found at

WEBSITE: www.kathyivan.com

**Follow Kathy on Facebook at
facebook.com/kathyivanauthor**

Follow Kathy on Twitter at twitter.com/@kathyivan

**Follow Kathy at BookBub
bookbub.com/profile/kathy-ivan**

DISCARD

Made in the USA
Las Vegas, NV
06 March 2021

19119090R00134